Bourbon Street

Bourbon Street

LEONCE GAITER

CARROLL & GRAF PUBLISHERS
NEW YORK

BOURBON STREET

Carroll & Graf Publishers
An Imprint of Avalon Publishing Group, Inc.
245 West 17th Street
New York, NY 10011

AVALON
publishing group incorporated

First Carroll & Graf edition 2005

Library of Congress Cataloging-in-Publication Data is available.

ISBN: 0-7867-1432-8

Printed in the United States of America
Interior design by Maria E. Torres
Distributed by Publishers Group West

To my father

Sometimes the world whispers to you, like too-young flesh too willing. You can almost feel the heat and wet of its tongue on your ear. Some believe it's God himself singling them out. But no god would so debase himself. No god would swivel his hips and moan and gyrate just for you. It's the world. It's the night. The unconscious yowl of a billion souls tramping toward their shocked, pain-wracked ends. Every now and then they swarm. The atmospheric conditions being just right, they join and momentarily rejoice in numbers, like a demon's hallelujah chorus, imps on an adrenaline rush, like a dust devil dancing on a dry Texas plain. Sometimes it comes your way.

It's called bad luck.

New Orleans, 1958

Chapter One

The bus was so loud he couldn't hear anything else. The big gears grinding, and then the broadening roar until the gears crunched again; it had sounded like a monster breathing ever since they'd hit the city. The whole ride from Texas he'd sat in the grimy back of this dingy bus, in the thick of the engine's dull roar, the dark window cut now and then by streaks of light as cars drove past or truck stops and small towns flashed by. As they approached New Orleans the big-city lights lunged like flashbulbs bursting—like a Hollywood premiere and a whole history of Fourths of July.

He hadn't known what to expect. He'd never been. It seemed impossible that a gambler could avoid New Orleans. But none had as good a reason as Deke; and then again, Deke was a gambler in name only. He only played games he could win. Sticking to the South and the Midwest, he picked his games carefully, gambled with suckers and almost always took their modest sums of money. He didn't seek the big-money games. He settled for the familiar and the middling and did quite nicely, thank you. As the bus hit the city he thought to himself, without lust or greed, *This game will be a beautiful thing.* These were the same folks he'd always played. Moneyed

amateurs or second-rate pros. These were simply richer. The
odds just didn't get any healthier than that.

The passengers stood in anticipation when the brakes
screeched the bus to a stop on Canal Street. A tall man, Deke
bent down to see out the windows. The stop was dark, but up
ahead were colors and motion bathed in light, shifting
shadows—indecipherable patterns twisting and swirling like
something inside a kaleidoscope.

A fat man in front of him heaved his huge bag up off the
ground and huffed and struggled his way to the front of the bus.
Big, florid, pink-faced, hauling a bag that must have weighed as
much as him, he yanked a white handkerchief out of his pocket
and mopped his sweating face. He dropped the bag with a thud
once he reached land and turned his full attention to his sweat.
He smeared it off his face and neck, then examined the handkerchief before folding it over to sop up some more.

Deke stepped out after him and stretched his back before he
picked up his bag and walked toward the brilliant, whirling
world up ahead. Right behind him, the fat man grunted as he
lifted his case. His heels clicked in time to his short, quick steps.

With his attention fixed on a tingling in his half-sleeping
foot, Deke turned a corner. Suddenly, a riotous swarm of men
and women surrounded him. They bore down on him like a
herd of beasts, as if he'd suddenly materialized in the midst of
a raucous parade. Horns blared ten different tunes, saxo-
phones and tubas and trumpets, while a hundred voices fought
to be heard. Sparklers sizzled and firecrackers smacked like
gunshots while boisterous laughter flew through the air like
bees, and bodies competed to see in how many different directions they could run and walk and scream and crawl. Their
elaborate and grotesque costumes ate up every square inch—
centaur heads of papier-mâché; kings and queens with foot-

tall wigs; red, naked, horned men; coffin-bearing pallbearers and mummified corpses shedding their rotting, linen skins. It was dizzying. Pushed from every side, Deke fought to stay in place and almost closed his eyes until the storm had passed.

And suddenly it had. No longer buffeted, he looked up to see that mass had passed him by; only a few stragglers were left behind.

The fat man walked up behind him. It was quiet enough to hear his labored breathing. That suitcase full of bricks hit the ground with its usual thud and what must have been one of many white handkerchiefs did duty on his round, shiny face.

"It's part of the religion, believe it or not," said the fat man, staring straight ahead.

Surprised, Deke looked over his shoulder to see if the man spoke to someone else.

"It's the days before Lent," he went on, examining his sweat. "That's when they have to abstain from things and quit doin' just about anything that's any fun."

After a pause and with a world-weary sigh, the man bent to pick up that tremendous suitcase. For the first time he looked at Deke.

"Before that, though," the man said, "before that they go just a little bit crazy." Leering a tight-lipped grin, he nodded at Deke and then resumed that quick-stepping dance with his colossal burden.

Deke noticed three colored men and two women standing around a fire burning in a barrel. It wasn't cold enough for it, but they stood there as if warming themselves against some nonexistent chill. And they were staring at him—really staring, as if they dared him to do something about it. He'd heard about this town. They said that colored folks didn't know their places here. Sure as hell in Texas no niggers would stare at a white man like that. They must have been damn sure of themselves to do it. Whatever made them so sure—whatever could make a nigger so sure to stare at a white man like that—was something he didn't want to mess with, not in this strange place where he'd already sensed that the rules had been discarded. So he did not confront them. He picked up his suitcase and made his way down Bourbon Street.

The French Quarter reminded Deke of a great big over-decorated wedding cake. The iron balconies had too many swirls and curlicues. The doors and windows had too many shutters. The shadows of too many ceiling fans skittered along the wooden porchlike floors that served as sidewalks. Deke was used to the bland American musk of Texas, not the prissy, Frenchified perfume that stank up the air around here. And these people. They hung out of every door and window, half of them in outlandish costume. Whores walked up and down the street as brazen as you please, not even a hint of shame, their smiles as big as sunshine as they minced along in spike heels, big thighs and dresses slit all the way up to there.

On top of all that, the streets were so narrow the two-story buildings seemed to lean in over you as if they could swallow you with one bite. Looking inside the strip clubs—the sidewalks in front of them dotted with huge posters of the half-naked "Busty" and "Ginger," while hard-drinking barkers yelled what the men really needed—Deke saw smoke so thick it looked like cinder blocks hung in the air. The horns again. You couldn't take another step without hearing more of those splatting, brassy horns. He knew that after a week in this place he'd give his eyeteeth to hear a fiddle. The noise blared through the open doors of one of the clubs. Inside, on the bandstand, four colored musicians played while a wild-haired, copper-colored man in a shiny suit stood up there with them,

"Sounds dangerous," replied Deke, taking the key.

"It is."

Deke stared at him a moment. No, he decided. He wasn't kidding.

"Call me Deke."

"Louisiana? Texas?" asked Ray, shaking the outstretched hand.

"Texas."

"It's all over your mouth." The clerk rang the bell to call a bellhop. "The name's Ray. Jimmy . . ."

The colored bellhop came and took Deke's case. The hop didn't wear a uniform, but his suit looked almost as good as Ray's. Deke followed the hop to the elevator, the iron cage of which was, of course, elaborately wrought.

Going up, Deke eyed the nigger in the shiny rich man's suit in the gilded cage with him and almost laughed out loud. The hop looked at him, just for an instant, but long enough and with enough hatred to make Deke remember to better guard his thoughts. As the elevator doors opened, Deke followed the hop down the hall. He realized that for the second time in as many hours, a look from a colored that should have demanded a white man's rightful response, had not.

The hop put the key in the door and swung it open. Deke walked into another lush, blood-red cocoon of a place, like he'd crawled up inside of some fat woman's belly. The dark woods and thick curtains looked as luxuriant and precious as everything downstairs.

"So how much is this gonna set me back," he said, almost to himself.

"Your bill's taken care of," the hop replied. "Mr. Moreau has seen to it."

Deke hadn't expected an answer, let along that one. For free, he could stand it. For free, he might even enjoy it a little, sit back and let that fat girl belch and fart—get a little comfortable.

Hands at his side, the hop still stood at the door. He wanted his tip, but he didn't perform any of the usual "make work" tics that bellhops use to signal a forgetful or ignorant guest. This one just stared, almost daring you not to give him his money. No. That wasn't it. He stared, knowing that you wouldn't dare *not* give him his money.

"Oh." Deke dug into his pocket and pulled out some change. He dropped the coins into the hop's waiting hand. The hop took it like a king's lieutenant taking tribute from a pauper: neither impressed by the sum, nor respectful enough of the source to have expected anything more. He shut the door quietly behind him.

Deke hadn't been alone for days. Buses and hotels and terminals and diners. He was tired of people's noises and smells. His little hotel rooms had always been a respite—home. Staring at ten feet by ten feet of dun-colored wallpaper, faded and cracked, with a picture of Jesus on the wall, Deke could imagine wide-open spaces and the freedom to move in any direction. No demands. But this busy place wouldn't give his eyes a rest. Lines and colors dragged them from here to there, insisting. He tried closing his eyes, to regain his sense of control. But he opened them, and . . . riot. Gold, red and green trails and patterns and gilt—all just for the sake of it.

He stepped onto the balcony and looked down at the amusement park of a street below. He'd been physically farther from where he belonged, but he'd never felt this foreign. The costumed creatures down on Bourbon Street looked like they belonged here. They reeked of enormous appetites tied to the promise of imminent satisfaction. That was a recipe for sinning. His preaching Papa had taught him that before he was ten. He'd spent a life staunching any appetite and avoiding the disappointment of what he'd been taught would be the inevitable failure to satisfy it.

Back in his room, he threw his suitcase on the bed. He opened it up and pulled out his things. A slightly frayed shirt collar seemed downright rude in the midst of all this tropical luxuriance. Beneath the shirt sat his snub-nosed .45. He'd never fired it. He didn't expect to. The gun was window dressing, a prop. He'd picked it up after the war, back when he expected to take his gambler's persona to heart. It hadn't worked out that way. He hadn't the skills or the temperament to make a true skin of it. It was just a child's mask with which he played hide-and-seek with the world. So far, he'd eluded detection. He just wasn't good enough, and he wasn't blessed with the idiocy required to delude himself that he was. Sometimes he was proud of that and sometimes it sickened him. A man forced to face himself ought at least to have some booby prize like they had on the TV for the folks who didn't win. Deke had to settle for the fact that he was not a fool. It was a mean, niggardly prize, and it didn't seem enough anymore.

He heard a lone horn. He figured he'd already been here too long because it sounded good to him. From his balcony, he saw a group gathering around the hornman down on Bourbon Street. Somehow, that one horn cut through all the noise and din. It was an aching song. The revelers slowed, took a moment and drank it in. When they walked away, they stepped a little less lightly, a bit more aware of the weight they tried so hard to ignore. Death took a few steps with them that night, until they could slough him off with a belt or a tickle about a half-block down.

A girl walked by in a yellow dress. She looked young, about sixteen or seventeen. It was one of those simple dresses, all of the same material, a belt cinching it at the waist—a girl's dress, not a woman's. Her dark blond hair fell onto her shoulders when she looked up and saw Deke. She leaned over and whispered to her girlfriend standing next to her. They both looked up and giggled.

Years ago, Deke had known a girl like her. Only she'd walked down a piss-poor Texas street, and there was no sadness on him yet. This town reminded him of what he'd done to her. She was one of his mistakes, and he lived with it still. That a small man like him had made so great a one . . . It always took him aback, like a bright diamond ring on a beggar's filthy hand. The hornman's song came to an end, and once more, the streamers flew and the voices screamed.

There was a knock on the door.

"Come in," Deke called, returning to the room.

The bellhop in the expensive suit walked in. Immediately, the hop's eyes scanned the room. He missed nothing. He even registered the frayed collars of Deke's shirts. And then he saw the gun exposed on the bed. His eyes lit up a bit. It was the first true sign of life he'd shown. Deke crossed to the bed and gathered up the gun. He put it back in his suitcase.

"They say these are just a quick end to a bad second act," he said, embarrassed. The hop just stood there, that same smirk on his face and a twinkling in his eyes.

"It's, uh . . . just for show. Gamblers are supposed to be tough guys." There was a pause.

"Of course," the hop replied. To Deke, the boy's voice didn't sound right. It didn't fit.

"It's not even loaded," Deke continued, unnecessarily.

"Really?" Jimmy replied.

Again, the voice didn't fit.

Deke took the gun out of the suitcase and looked around

for an appropriate place to stash it, one that would meet with the colored hop's approval. He dove for the chifforobe and put it in the top drawer. When he turned around, he was staring down the barrel of a gun held by the colored bellhop in the rich man's silk suit.

"This one is," the hop said.

A mallet slammed Deke in the chest. His heart skipped beats. He stopped breathing. Jimmy smiled. Seeing the arrant shock on Deke's face, he seemed satisfied and put the gun back inside his jacket.

"Once you've settled yourself," he said in his beautiful voice, "there's a small reception for the members of the game party in the lounge." He turned to leave. Deke figured out what it was. It wasn't just the quality of his voice; it was the diction, the poise of it.

"You . . . uh . . ." he had to remember to breathe "talk awfully fine for a colored man," he said, surprised—surprised that he fought for breath to say *that*, of all things, to a nigger who had just held a gun on him.

"It's *well*, Mr. Watley," the hop said, a smile on his face. "Awfully *well*."

He closed the door behind him.

Chapter Two

After taking time to put his pride back in place, Deke changed his shirt and prepared to meet his foes. In the lobby, Ray pointed him down the rococo hallway to a set of carved mahogany double doors. Since the bellhop incident, he felt like he was running a gauntlet, as if a series of trials had been laid before him to test his mettle. God must have figured that Deke needed a goose. All he could do was cover his ass the best he could and scoot on ahead just a little bit faster.

His hands on both cold, copper doorknobs, he breathed deeply as he drew the remarkably heavy doors toward him. At least there'd be no cripples in this group, he thought. They'd never get in.

Although the size of your average house, the room bore the air of a well-appointed study. It had the coldness he always associated with the rich, but also the excess that people with too much money mistook for warmth. A woman sprawled on the brown leather sofa; a man stood behind it. At an ornately carved sideboard a man with his back to the door craned his neck to get a good look at the newcomer. Holding a shoe in one hand while her other grasped a corn-infested foot sat an older woman, also stock-still and staring. A frail-looking man seated in a high-backed chair was chewing on his nails. They all looked professionally posed, as if waiting for the flash to pop before they moved. It took them a moment, but they finally came to life. A smile, bright and phony as pyrite, lit up the reclining woman's face. The man behind her scooted from behind the sofa he used like a shield. A smile wormed its way over his mouth as he extended his hand.

"Ah. You must be Mr. Watley."

Deke couldn't place the accent. It was either British or ridiculous. He wasn't worldly enough to tell the difference.

"Call me Deke," he replied.

The man turned to look at the others, his audience. "Call me *Ishmael*," he announced as he shook Deke's hand and chortled merrily. The others looked to one another for reassurance before they, too, forced laughs as hearty and urbane as the man's. The reclining woman looked disgusted.

"What?" Deke asked, half to her and half to himself.

The man laughed even louder. He finally let go of Deke's hand to slap a thigh with mirth. Having had enough, the woman rose from her leather perch. She approached Deke and shook his hand.

"Pritchett read a book once," she said, indicating the laughing man, who now shook his head and held up his hands in an "I'm sorry, just couldn't resist" gesture. The others seemed relieved that they didn't have to laugh anymore and abruptly stopped.

"I'm Stacy," the woman continued. "Laughing boy here is Pritchett, my husband." She pointed to the woman now putting her shoe back on. "This is Honey." Honey gave a little wave. Next came the little man chewing his hands. "Barker," she said of him. Finally taking his hand from his mouth, he nodded.

The man at the bar had a hard-core face. Not hard-core

anything in particular, just hard-core. Anything he shouldn't have done he'd done too much of and liked too well. "Tate," she said. He turned back to finish making his drink.

"Howdy," Deke said to the group.

"Sit, sit. Tell us about yourself," Pritchett prompted.

Deke took a seat and grabbed hold of the armrests when he saw the silk-suited, gun-toting bellhop enter with a tray of drinks. The hop walked straight to Deke.

"Bourbon and seven?" he asked.

"That's the usual," Deke replied.

"Here you are." As polite as could be, Jimmy placed a white napkin on the table and set the drink down next to Deke.

"How'd you know?" Deke asked.

"We know a lot about you, Deke," Pritchett replied.

Deke picked up the drink. "You should tell me about me sometime," he said as he took a sip. "I thought I wanted scotch." These people were starting to piss him off, and only the lady, Stacy, had the sense to know it. Pritchett was like a cat with a lizard. He'd go as far as you'd let him. The other three looked variously bored or drunk. The colored bellhop seemed more at ease here than they did.

"Talk to us, honey," the older woman said, and Deke suddenly knew why they called her Honey.

"Nothin' to tell," he replied. "I'm just . . . a gambler."

"Ah," Pritchett said, shaking the lizard by the tail, "a simple man. That usually means he's either annoyingly soulful or incredibly stupid."

Deke stared at him. "Like with most men," he replied, "that depends on the quality of the liquor."

"Where *is* Alex?" said Stacy, squelching the fight her husband was picking. And as if on cue, the huge doors swung open and in walked Alexander Moreau. Deke wasn't surprised.

Which tells you how far he'd come in just one evening. Young, maybe twenty, maybe thirty. The power said thirty, but the boyish face said much younger. He was colored, like the people out on the street, but he was mixed. He had that copper-orange skin and wavy black hair like so many colored down here. Deke almost dropped his drink when he realized this was the man from the bandstand on Bourbon Street, the one who played the piano that wasn't there.

"Fashionably late as usual, Stacy," he said as he marched into the room. Everyone's nerves stood up straight. Deke could feel the hair on their necks rise. They'd been bored and distracted before, but Alex now commanded their undivided attention. He had Deke's too. There was something wild about him. In the eyes, the mouth. He was beautiful. Looking at him, you knew that there was only one like him in this world, and you didn't know how such an oddity behaved (what, pray tell, were its habits, its mores, its pet peeves) and that scared you, but you couldn't take your eyes off of him. Alex rubbed his hands together as he looked around the room.

"Let the games begin," he said. "Jimmy." The bellhop almost stood at attention. He'd long ago abandoned his silver serving tray and leaned against the wall to enjoy the show. "You're wanted." Quickly grabbing his tray, he demurely left the room and closed the huge doors ceremoniously behind him.

"Alex Moreau," he said, extending a hand to Deke.

"Deke Watley." Deke was surprised he was already standing. He couldn't remember when he'd gotten to his feet.

"You're a wicked poker player, Deke. When I read about the Dallas win, I knew I wanted you here."

Alex moved to the sideboard. Tate, the hard-core, stepped aside as he approached.

"You're not what I expected," Alex continued, mixing. "You don't look rich enough for these stakes."

It wasn't insulting. Not from him. The way he said it, you knew that only a fool would not have mentioned it, and only a bigger one would have taken offense.

Deke looked him in the eye. "I can handle it," he said.

With an almost imperceptible flick of the head, Alex signaled that Deke's word was all he needed and went on. "Every few years we invite the winner of a regional. Keeps us on the ball, playing with pros. You know we play five card, one-hundred dollar ante, and we play 'til we drop. It's a day game, due to the festivities."

It was like watching a show. Every gesture, every movement was effortlessly constructed to manipulate his audience. The drink he held seemed to have flown into his hand. You couldn't remember him making it.

"Sounds like it does get pretty rich," Deke said.

"You want to be rich, Deke?" He had the strangest way of introducing dissonance. It threw Deke, and everyone else. Not knowing how to answer the question without playing the patsy, Deke just shrugged.

"Two-fisted greed," gauged Alex, eyeing Deke's confusion. "You'll do nicely."

"You folks know all about me," Deke said, "but I don't know nothin' about you." It was time for some information. If the game had begun, he was already behind.

"Well, let's see . . ." said Alex, looking around the room. "Uh . . . Pritchett here is my father's lawyer, and we're still not sure where he bought the degree." There were weak smiles all around. Everyone tried to pretend it was in good fun. "His wife Stacy sits all alone at night, don't you, Stace, baying at the moon and waiting for the fleet to dock." She rose from the sofa and stood by the window, staring out. Everyone, including Deke, braced himself for whatever might come. "Honey here is the city's finest madame and previously one of its foremost whores."

"Your father," interjected Pritchett, playing his trump, "wouldn't appreciate you perverting this . . ."

"I need another drink," Tate drawled drunkenly, smashing Pritchett's moment.

"And what are you, Alex?" Stacy turned back to the room, her courage up. Alex smiled. He seemed to like a little backbone.

Barker tried to inch his way out of his seat. "I . . . I've got some work to do," he managed to say through a mouthful of his own fingers.

"SHUT UP. Sit down." Alex's contempt splattered the walls as if he'd heaved offal about the place. They all stood there dripping in it. For a moment, all the play was gone from him.

"Come on, Alex," Stacy ventured, "What are you?"

The smile crept back into Alex. "I," he said, the smile reaching his lips, "am . . . "—he took a long pause "—mis-under-*stood*."

Like a true showman, Alex took the moment, and then threw himself into an oversized leather chair.

"Did you know, ladies and gentlemen," he said, looking at Deke and sending a chill through him. "Did you know that this man here is a bona fide killer?"

Barker even stopped chewing his nails.

"Really now!" said Stacy, barely able to contain her excitement.

Deke stared at Alex. "That's a lie."

"Did it with his bare hands, too."

"Self-defense," Deke spat.

"True. He was cleared. But the man did not come back to

life once the verdict was read. He remains quite dead. That means you still killed him."

Now, for the first time since Alex walked in the room, Deke saw colored. He saw a nigger sitting there calling him a killer.

"How dare you, you little—"

Alex's eyes had been riveted to Deke's. He rose and moved so quickly and softly he might have floated right up to him. "How dare I what?"

Out of the corner of his eye, Deke saw Barker actually lower his head into his hand to cover his eyes. Stacy had stopped breathing. The whole room screamed at him to stop. Alex's eyes, inches from his, urged "Come on . . . You know you want to . . ." Deke was not a stupid man.

"I am not a killer," he said. Alex actually looked disappointed, as if he was looking forward to what might have been if Deke had taken the bait.

"Don't get defensive," said Alex, returning to his seat. "We won't throw you out of the game for it. Actually, it's all the more reason to keep you in it. If there's one thing, and one thing only, that we won't tolerate, it's moral superiority."

Everyone laughed a hearty, tension-easing laugh. Alex stared at Deke like a jockey stares at a prize-winning horse. Deke wanted to turn off the gaze. It was too hungry, too keen. As the laughter died, the double doors swung open. A man in a black suit stood there solicitously holding the arm of a powerful-looking, sixtyish man. The older man wore dark glasses, and it took Deke a moment to realize he was blind. Alex retired to the sideboard to mix a drink. He turned his back to the doorway.

Surprised and delighted, Pritchett leapt from his seat. "August," he said, grabbing the man's hand to pump it vigorously. "Good to see you."

"I couldn't let my game begin without a visit," said the man, full of pride.

"August began this game many years ago," Stacy purred.

"Our guest?" August inquired.

"Yes. Deke, come." Pritchett gesticulated and stage-managed to plop Deke in the proper position. "Deke Watley, this is August Moreau."

If he'd been playing for his life, Deke would have been a dead man. This blind, white man was Alex's father. Deke's eyes shot to Alex, who made a little "Surprise!" gesture with his hands.

"Say something," Moreau said good-naturedly.

"It's . . . uh, good to meet you."

"Alex has mentioned your skills. Is Alex here?"

Arms folded, drink in hand, he was leaning against the sideboard, staring at the group.

"Right here," said Pritchett, finally enjoying some all-too-rare payback. "As a matter of fact, we were just talking about you, weren't we, Alex?"

All eyes turned to him. Stacy and Pritchett obviously enjoyed his retreat into silence. "Alex?" Pritchett repeated.

He just stood, watching them.

"Alex," his father said.

At that he plunged his hand into the bucket's half-melted ice. The loose cubes clacked and clattered. He dropped three into his glass. Clink . . . clink . . . clink . . .

August Moreau stood impassive as he took the insult. He turned to the others with a salesman's excuse for a smile on his face. "I wish you all a wonderful and profitable game. I must go. Deke, good luck to you."

"Thank you, sir."

Moreau paused a moment. His blind eyes haunted the direction of his son's noise. "Goodnight Alex," he said. Even the fake smile had disappeared. Moreau stood there, waiting, fury pouring off of him like smoke. Everyone else sat motionless, and Deke couldn't tell which scared him most, the father or the son. Either could have pulled a gun and killed the other right there, and it would not have surprised him. Finally, the servant rushed to take Moreau's arm as he turned to leave.

Alex sat in a corner, an attitude befitting the naughty child he'd been reduced to. No one spoke. No one moved. In the oppressive quiet, the doors sounded like a vault slamming shut.

"We should be off, too," Stacy finally braved, with a triumphant glance at Alex. "It was a pleasure meeting you, Deke."

All the others rose and said their good-byes. Tate, drunk, stumbled. Barker yanked his bloodied fingers from his mouth just in time to catch him. The last one out, Honey shut the doors behind her. Deke was alone with Alex, which might have been the last place in the world he wanted to be.

"Well . . . I better . . ."

"He owns this place. I run it, and they're here to keep an eye on me. This place, it's my toy. Something he gives me to shut me up."

That just about answered all Deke's questions, and he found himself grateful to the younger man for acknowledging the legitimacy of his curiosity and doing him the courtesy of not making him ask. Alex's manner had changed. He'd dropped the cat-and-canary routine. He opened the window as he looked out. Only a set of wrought iron bars separated them from the frantic street revelries.

"You ever been to Mardi Gras?" he shouted to Deke over the din of the bewigged and costumed crowds outside.

"No."

"It gets wild sometimes. Wild, I tell you. Scary even."

"Seems pretty wild now."

"Each day it gets more manic, more frenzied, until finally you know it's all got to blow. Fire. Madness. Like something out of hell."

Deke began to sincerely entertain the prospect that Alex was insane. He thought it best to change the subject.

"Must be nice, you gettin' to run this place. You bein' . . ." Deke couldn't believe he almost said it. Like most white people when trying to be polite, Deke thought it was insulting to acknowledge Alex was colored but would have called him a nigger at the drop of a hat. To Deke, there was so little difference, and he assumed that the two were synonymous to Alex as well.

Alex closed the window. He turned from it, and stared Deke straight in the eye. "I'd leave tomorrow if I wouldn't be living in a shotgun shack and walking in through someone's back door."

Deke pretended to understand what he thought he should but didn't. "I guess," he replied.

"You should go out and take a look around, Deke. Most people don't see this in a lifetime."

Deke looked out the window. "Think I will."

Alex downed the rest of his drink and headed for the door. "You like music, dancing?" he asked offhandedly.

"Sure," Deke replied.

"You might try the Ten Spot," said Alex, opening the doors, his back to Deke. "That's a good place. On Lafayette, down by the river." He paused a moment, and then strode through the door. Deke watched him recede down that blood-red hallway.

Chapter Three

Out of the French Quarter's fray, the world grew quiet. The dark, gothic streets reeked of grandeur and ruin. The past crawled all over the city like insects on a carcass. Gargantuan magnolias allowed to run riot boasted shoots and branches that created house-sized structures of their own. With their big, shiny green leaves and soon to hold huge white blossoms they seemed primordial, and both mocked and accessorized the inhabitants' desperate attempt to mimic their permanence.

Deke passed a cemetery. He'd never seen anything like it. Great tombs decorated with saints and gargoyles struck in stone sat on slabs above the ground. These people couldn't even die like everyone else, he thought. Not content to be placed in the ground, they had to sit above it, to tower in stone among the living.

He'd stopped paying attention to where he was going and got himself quite lost. He didn't want to go back, though. For the first time since he'd hit town he'd found a little peace. There was very little here. Just some old buildings, factories maybe down by the great, big river. Nothing fancy. For once, nothing fancy. When he saw the sign he laughed. Up the street, a sign on a shacklike place read, TEN SPOT BAR. What the hell, he thought. He needed a drink.

It was dark inside. There was a bar alongside the far wall. There was a jukebox, and in a little dance area a woman in a black cocktail dress danced with a gray-suited man to the strains of Dinah Washington—"Blue Gardenia." Deke liked the song and he liked the place. Each table even had a little candle on it. He took a seat at the bar.

"What can I get you?" the colored barkeep asked.

"Bourbon and sev . . . No. Make that a scotch. I'm gettin' predictable." The bartender didn't crack a smile. Good, Deke thought. No-nonsense drinking here.

The song on the jukebox ended, and the man and the woman stopped dancing. Each set the other free without even a glance. No-nonsense everything, Deke noted. The woman headed to the juke and stood with both hands on it; slipping free of one black shoe, she rubbed the calf of her shapely leg with the top of her foot. She had a good figure. Dark blonde hair fell thickly to just below her shoulders. It had that slightly wild, unkempt look that Deke had always liked.

She stood there a long time studying the selections. Finally she rested on one outstretched arm as she pushed the buttons. It surprised him when something so slow came on. A woman like that, he expected something lively. Instead, the same notes again and again—could have been a piano or a guitar, he couldn't tell—and then some horns played a sad, sad tune. She walked to the screened door and looked outside at the silent night. She stretched and put her hands beneath the fall of her hair to raise it off her neck. It could have been the walk or it could have been the gesture, but as she headed for the bar, Deke turned away. Fairy tales didn't come true, and if they did, you'd pay, he knew. For deliverance from what he'd come to this town not daring to admit he ever wanted, for what every god and hell knew he didn't deserve, there would be a price. He felt her coming closer. Two seats down she leaned over the bar. She barely gestured, but the bartender brought her a drink. She looked at Deke. He couldn't even turn his head enough to see her out of the corner of his eye. His heart beat faster. He looked for a door that wouldn't take him past her. If there had been one, he would have run through it.

She was staring at him. He knew that. Then she moved closer. He could smell her—part perfume, part makeup, part hair.

"Hey," he heard her low voice right behind him. "You dance?"

Hoping he was wrong, he sat wondering if he could turn around and be wrong. Slowly, he turned on his stool toward her and looked up into her still beautiful face.

It's fascinating to watch a face dissolve. Hers bore a look of feminine mastery the moment he saw it, and then, when she saw his, that studied look liquified into masks of horror and hurt and hatred that took turns melting into one another in chaotic patterns over which she had no control. She turned, grabbed her purse and ran toward the door. At her first step Deke was out of his seat and after her. She was halfway there when he grabbed her arm and turned her toward him. There were tears in her eyes. She tried to yank her arm away from him. She pushed at him with her other hand, but he held on tight.

Then her body slumped. The will and the fight dissolved and left her smaller, frail. He barely heard her sobs as he put his hand on her hair and laid her head against his shoulder. That slow, sad music still played. He kissed her hair and holding her, swayed to the music.

* * * *

Alex strode through the hotel restaurant, his silver silk suit blazing. Black and white waiters and busboys with trays perched high swerved thoughtlessly to let him pass. All of the diners knew who he was. The son of August Moreau. Moreau's nigger bastard. Black New Orleanians feared and resented him; white New Orleanians feared and hated him. For August had let it be known: He would kill any man who touched his son. And August did not just kill. August ripped and savaged. Tales of his vengeance were legend, and all had been warped to emphasize the exquisite pain, the downright operatic agonies, in which his victims had died. He'd kept a lower profile since turning up blind, but no one forgot. He saw to that.

Alex was a lot like his father. "If he'd a been white," they all said, "he'd a been king of this town." As it stood, Alex was king of L'Hotel Moreau. Black folks knew he went too far. They knew they suffered because of the liberties he took—acting like some white man, flaunting his enforced inviolability. They knew they were demeaned and brutalized more often by whites desperate to get the taste of that vicious, uppity nigger out of their mouths. The Creoles, the quadroons and all the other high-yellow coloreds resented the fact that they weren't good enough for him. Their smart society wasn't smart enough. Their privilege wasn't privileged enough. He wouldn't stop, they said, until he had everything—until he was downright white.

Walking through the restaurant, Alex saw Barker heading in his direction. Barker turned to avoid being seen. When he finally lifted his eyes off of his wingtips, he almost jumped out of his skin to find Alex right in front of him. Alex lifted his hand. Barker flinched, but Alex just helpfully tucked Barker's shirt collar under his jacket lapel. Barker's fingernails flew to his mouth as if magnetized and attracted to teeth.

"I want Watley to win tomorrow," Alex said. Barker's head immediately shook back and forth like a child's.

"I can't fix the game," he said. "Mr. Moreau . . . Your father would—"

"My father . . ." Alex interrupted, "is not here. I am, Barker. And I can *see* you." Barker nodded.

"And he'll continue winning until I say otherwise," Alex continued as he straightened and fiddled with Barker's jacket. From Barker's reaction he might have been sticking pins in him.

"Subtly, Barker," Alex continued. "Nothing obvious. You're very good when you want to be."

"Yes, sir."

At a nearby table sat Don Boudrille out of Plaquemine, Louisiana. A hardware man, he'd brought his wife down to see the Mardi Gras. He was a little shocked to see colored and white folks sitting in the same restaurant. But this was New Orleans. They had whores all up and down the streets, and half the city was dressed up like it had lost its mind. Things were different here during Carnival, that's all. Wasn't that why he'd opted for New Orleans this vacation—the tickle of wickedness?

He'd been watching Alex. That suit and the way he walked and the way white men moved out of his way. Now, not five feet away, a white man was calling him "Sir."

* * * *

She'd been sixteen years old and the kindest thing he'd ever known. The woman sitting in front of Deke was not the same. He knew that; but it didn't matter. She didn't have to be. She was one of his mistakes. How many men have a chance to make those right?

He talked. Told her why he'd come to New Orleans, what

had happened so far. He said that there had to be some kind of fate for him to find her here.

She looked so much the same, Deke thought. She looked the same.

"No one'd ever been that good to me before. Or since," he said, remembering.

"Then why'd you leave?"

"I saw a girl who looked like you today. She reminded me of that."

"Answer me."

The sudden steel surprised him. He wished to God he had a better answer. "Young, I guess. Stupid. I thought I could . . . I don't know . . . I don't know . . . "

"Be somebody?" she asked, fingering the little red candle on the table.

"Yeah," he replied, feeling the sting. "Be somebody." He paused. "I'm still workin' on that. I got a chance here. This game I'm in. I can win big. This could set me up for a long, long time." He was surprised to hear himself consider big winnings. Seeing her again, he wanted them.

She looked up at him. "I hope it happens for you."

"I can't believe I found you here."

"I've been worse places." She stood suddenly and grabbed her purse. "Let's get out of here."

She took him outside, and they walked down the dark and empty streets. She took him down by the river. She stopped to stare out at the lights of the ferry heading to the other side. Then she kept on walking. Deke did all the talking. He thought words might keep her.

"Everybody in this town knows too much about me, and I don't know a damn thing about anyone. You haven't said a word about yourself. What you been doin' all this time?"

She shrugged. "Best I can."

"I mean are you married? You in love?"

She laughed at that. "Deke Watley talking about love. That's a change. When did you become the romantic?"

"I'm gettin' old," Deke said. "I've tried everything else."

"I'm not married," she answered. "I'm not in love. I've just been drifting. Some good luck. Some bad. For a long time now, the good's had a way of turning bad for me." She took a cigarette from her purse. He lit it for her.

"No, no," Deke protested, smiling and shaking his head. "You were so good . . . and so beautiful. Everyone said so. When'd you start talking like that?"

She stopped and stared straight ahead. There was no distance between using him and the truth. "After you left," she said.

He marveled at how one act, one tiny scene of his life, had come to dominate it so fully. He didn't realize that it—that act—was just the spark that lit combustibles that had been seeping for years. Witnessing wars small and large, inside and between his mother and father, nations; praising Jesus and dreading damnation under the covers at night and all the while becoming dismayed at the prospect of living in this world and desperately clutching any excuse not to. He had had a chance to change all that, to step out of the battlefield grave-yard that had come to embody the world to him, and he had let it go.

He didn't fight it. He let the guilt and longing overwhelm him. He took her arm, and when he couldn't stand the hard, empty look in her eyes, he pulled her close and held her tight, as if trying to take her into himself, to absorb whatever it was his mistake had become—to make it right.

* * * *

Don Boudrille pulled his napkin from his chin and threw it on the table.

"Did you hear that?" he thundered to his wife and everyone else. "A white man callin' a nigger 'sir'? "

"Don," his wife embarrassedly admonished as all eyes turned to them. Boudrille stood and stared at Alex and Barker.

Ray's desk sat at the opposite end of a long, grand hallway from the restaurant. A uniformed bellhop hung around the station.

"Call an ambulance," Ray told him.

"I don't like no white men callin' niggers 'sir'," Boudrille announced to the restaurant. A couple of diners tried to pretend it hadn't happened, but that only lasted a moment. The tinkle and clatter of silver on china ceased entirely.

Alex sighed and stared at the ordinary-looking, red-faced white man. The poor thing had no idea. He couldn't fathom that he'd entered an alternate universe in which Alex, and Alex alone, held sway. He couldn't fathom what Alex did to keep it that way. Alex had learned from the awe that white folks inspired in colored ones. Black folks stood in awe of those who had raped and murdered and butchered them. He often lamented that there had been so little white blood shed. He knew. It had osmosed through the warm, red goo in his mother's black womb, swum into him on the back of his white father's seed. He knew that if all those colored women taking care of all those white babies had, one night, after girding themselves, killing their Jesus, whispering plans among themselves for days, months, years—if they had one night resurrected their ancient gods of death and vengeance and quietly, mercilessly, smashed the brains out of those tiny, defenseless creatures who'd never done them any harm (this time white mothers waking to blood and madness, white men breathless at the viciousness)—if they had, Alex knew, one way or another Don Boudrille would not be standing before him calling him a nigger. The black and white of him knew it.

Alex turned without casting another eye on Boudrille and disappeared into the bowels of the restaurant. Jimmy appeared and stood at Boudrille's right. A quick, lascivious grin flew on and off of Barker's face as he positioned himself on the man's left side. Each of them placed one hand on Boudrille's arm and planted the other in his armpit. He felt their grips tighten. As he shifted slightly, he sensed he could not move. His look of surprise brought his wife to her feet.

"We'll take him to the manager, ma'am. He can make a complaint," Barker assured her.

At that, Boudrille was practically lifted off of his feet. Struggling in earnest now, he refused to believe he was being dragged through the restaurant. He wanted to shout out his protest, but he couldn't. His position was so absurd, so helpless. It infuriated him to the point of speechlessness. His face was the first thing to hit the swinging double doors into the kitchen. Cooks and sous chefs calmly stepped out of the way.

"What the hell is this!?" he finally screamed, just as his head ran past the gauntlet of pots hanging from the ceiling. He saw a dim, narrow hallway before him and another set of doors. He thrashed violently. He kicked and hollered. He closed his eyes as his face pounded through the doors; and then he was free and falling.

He landed flat on his face. Slime on the ground kept him from planting his hands firmly enough to lift his dazed self up, so he stayed there a moment to get his bearings. It was garbage. He was outside, in some kind of alley, and there was garbage all over the ground.

"I'll kill you," he heard himself mutter. Flies buzzed murderously and the rotting stench overwhelmed him in the still, humid night air.

"Welcome to customer relations," he heard a voice say. He looked up and saw Alex standing at the other end of the alleyway, his figure perfectly framed by brick walls on either side and a sliver of moon in the sky.

"They'll kill you for this," he said.

"That's doubtful," Alex replied.

"You can't do this!" insisted Boudrille, pounding his fist in the dirt.

"You had a complaint," Alex coached impatiently.

"I don't talk to—" Boudrille stopped himself.

"Ah. There it is. You were about to call me something, weren't you?"

Alex approached him and touched his cheek with the tip of his shoe. "I could tell."

"Niggers," Boudrille spat. "I don't talk to niggers." He lay on the ground and waited for the worst. He waited. He waited.

Alex had produced a file and engrossed himself in digging some foreign substance from beneath his left index fingernail. He wanted the man nervous. He wanted his audience, Jimmy and Barker, nervous. The way they would tell of this was all that mattered. "Oh, pardon me," he said. "My mind wandered. What was that?"

Again, the white man weighed his options.

"Nigger," he spat into the mud and stared at Alex's shoes.

"Speak up," Alex said, a sudden anger welling up in him. "Don't mumble!"

The man's face turned beet-red. Spittle flew and he shook with rage as he screamed, "NIGGER! I CALLED YOU A NIGGER!"

Alex's foot reared back and kicked the face like it was a tin can. All heard the snapping sound and saw the blood gush out of Boudrille's mouth. Jimmy watched impassively. Barker flinched as the foot met the flesh, but his repugnance lost the fight with his lurid fascination.

"I don't think he's a very nice man at all," Alex told Jimmy and Barker. The creature on the ground was no longer human to him. It was not animal. It was just flesh and mass.

Filthy and bleeding, Boudrille still asserted his privilege. "I doe taw to nehus!" he wept through blood and teeth and bone. As opposed to the placid lesson Alex had planned to teach, he found himself enraged. The smell of freedom made any reminder of his imprisonment all the more foul. He could taste the day when he would never have to suffer men like this, so Don Boudrille became a symbol. He was every black or white man he'd had to beat, or threaten or kill to get what would have been handed to any white man on a platter. This poor fool had just called the wrong man "nigger."

Barker closed his eyes. Even Jimmy flinched as Alex walked from place to place as if in a trance, then set himself and kicked the man's face again, and then stepped deliberately to another spot from which to smash that face again, and then another, and again, and again. To any onlooker, he seemed to plan his angles as carefully as any portraitist plans his brushstrokes—in the throes of bloody creation. Bone cracked. Flesh tore. His rage was ruled by parts of the brain most men have the luxury to ignore.

When he finally looked down at what he'd done, even he was shocked at what was left. The man was still conscious. His breathing was irregular. He made sounds like whimpers. He could not speak through the lips that looked as if knives had been taken to them, or see through the eye that dangled from its socket, or breathe through the nose that almost lay flat against his blood-drenched face.

"Get him out of here," said Alex, recovering from his exertions and shocked at his loss of control.

Barker and Jimmy moved to pick him up, but didn't quite know how. Where to place their hands to produce the least pain? At what point would he not break?

"Blood *disgusts* me!" muttered Alex, wiping spots of the stuff from his suit as he stormed inside.

* * * *

Down the street from Deke and Hannah, Tate, too, thought a cigarette sounded good, so he lit one. Not only did he need a smoke, he had to take a piss. Turning to face a wall, he craned his neck to keep an eye on his quarry. He happened to spy Deke and Hannah on his way back from a bottle blonde. Stacy hated Hannah, and he knew she'd pay dearly for all the details. He worked for Moreau but took some gravy on the side whenever he could. A man did what a man had to do. He thought of Stacy as he pulled his penis from his trousers. This bit might even get him another shot at her. The very idea made him stiffen a little. A man like him didn't get a classy piece like that every day. Even here, alone, he waved his big dick around before settling down to urinate. He was so used to brandishing it in urinals and attracting the envious stares of other men that he couldn't piss without a flourish. He sighed as he let lose a massive stream against the building, while he watched Deke and Hannah down the street a ways.

* * * *

The diners glanced only furtively when Alex returned. They wanted to know, and they didn't want to know. They had seen enough to imagine. That was good enough for Alex's needs. They would hear tell. The whole town would know and tomorrow would stand in awe at what he'd done.

"Excuse me, ma'am," Alex said to Mrs. Boudrille, practically clicking his heels in formal abjection. "Your husband decided against returning. He suggested you meet him by the side of the hotel."

The woman looked flustered as she rose. Grabbing her gloves and purse, she looked around for any sundries that may have escaped her.

"Thank you so much," she said to Alex. She opened her purse and pulled out a tip, which he accepted with a smart bow.

"Thank you, ma'am." The smile on his face disappeared the moment her back was turned. Still chiding himself for his lack of control in the alley, he passed a busboy.

"Here," he said, dropping the change into the boy's hand without so much as glancing at him. "Buy yourself some land."

Outside, the wild cry of an ambulance approached the hotel.

Chapter Four

Alex hated this house. He shook his head each time he caught sight of it as he passed the rich men's houses on Bellaire Drive. He was regularly amazed at its dreadfulness. As he cruised up its long, arced driveway, he slowed his car to watch the clouds and moonlight play menacingly above it; he practically expected organ music to blare out in gothic accompaniment. After Alex's mother died, his father didn't so much build this house as tear down the last one. The building-up was an after-thought. "Oh," he realized, "I'll need a place to live." He bought himself an architect with an expensive name to create this hideous mass of overlapping planes, like enormous razors suspended in air with some mysterious, malignant purpose. Only when you got up close did you see the windows that passed for walls. It reminded Alex of a modern take on the pharaohs' mausoleums. It was his father as Cheops, only Moreau had moved in while *waiting* to die. He had, however, dragged his vassals and valuables with him. Alex was just one among them.

The house was always steeped in blind man's darkness. Walking through the front door, you entered a room the size of a basketball court. The far side led to the hall, off which the bedrooms lay. To the right, was the dining room, with its large, inviting bar. Alex poured himself a drink, parked on a stool and stared off into the cavernous emptiness of his father's architectural folly. In the huge living room sat only a slablike sofa and couple of chairs, dwarfed and huddled together as if for warmth before the enormous fireplace.

A German shepherd lifted its massive head off its paws. Moreau's hand was lying on the dog, and the animal's movement woke him.

"Hannah?" called Moreau, anticipatory. He dozed in his ornate silk dressing gown. In this cavernous place with its modern furnishings, he might have arisen from a coroner's slab. Alex mumbled a curse to himself. If he had seen his father there, he would not have stopped at the bar.

"Alex," Moreau said resignedly.

Alex downed his drink.

"I hope the game goes well," said Moreau, standing. "You found a good man?"

"He'll do nicely."

Moreau walked toward the hallway. His dog rose to follow. He stopped after a moment.

"I often try to picture you," he said, "but I can't. Seeing you . . . it was so long ago. And I never mastered the blind man's touch."

"And what would be different if you could see me?" Alex asked perfunctorily.

"You might be more real. A person instead of a . . . a reminder."

Alex's foot tapped furiously against the bar. He dunked his hand in the ice bucket. Once again he slowly threw three cubes into his glass. Clink . . . Clink . . . Clink.

"You can treat me as if I don't exist in this house. I don't care," Moreau said, anger rising. "But never in public, do you understand? Never!" He turned to leave the room.

"Or what?" Alex said. His father stiffened at the challenge. Alex suddenly flailed his arms toward the dog and snarled like a madman at it. It lunged viciously.

"Heel!" Moreau shouted. The dog instantly obeyed.

"Like mother, like son?" Alex leered.

"Come." Moreau turned and continued down the hallway. Alex finished his drink and poured himself another. He knew he had nothing to lose. It wouldn't be long now.

* * * *

Alex had been right. It got wilder. It looked as if madmen were tearing things apart outside the hotel. The frenzy, the noise and the fires all raged. Standing naked by his balcony doors, Deke stared in awe at the chaos below. He saw a woman teasing several men, but they were getting rough. She tried to ease them back to the tease, but one of them grabbed her breast and then her crotch, and then her nails clawed red marks down his face. The man slapped her hard and knocked her down. The men all laughed.

Hannah's hands touched his back. He felt her breasts against him as she slipped her arms around him. He turned toward her and felt his skin on hers. He put his mouth against hers and drank her lips and tongue and let his fingers feel her flesh, gently, gently, as if he might break her yet again.

* * * *

With great relief, Ray quickly stamped out his cigarette at the knock on the door of his L'Hotel Moreau suite.

"You're an hour late," he said coldly.

"Sorry."

Ray stood aside to let the handsome young man in. Carl looked sheepish, and a little guilty. Ray liked that. It meant he must consider him human.

Carl's eyes darted here and there to avoid the masked ravages of Ray's face. He never said much. This time, he walked directly to the bedroom. After a moment, Ray followed.

Ray crossed to the small writing desk and lowered himself into the chair. As Carl took off his shoes and socks, Ray noted the arch of his foot. When Carl removed his shirt, Ray remarked the elegant line of downy hair that flowed from his navel. Carl removed his pants, and Ray admired the movement of the muscles beneath the skin on his thighs. It all reminded Ray of what the body, unmarred, was like. The glory of the form when whole.

Once naked, Carl felt a little absurd standing there in front of a masked man who sat impassively in pants and a robe, watching him. He started fidgeting with his clothes, folding them and straightening them.

"I'm not gonna take this thing off. You can look at me."

Carl straightened up, but did not turn toward him.

"LOOK AT ME!"

Carl finally turned. Ray opened a desk drawer and pulled some bills from it. He threw them on the desk, then rose and took off his robe. Carl was unable to keep from eyeing Ray's beautifully muscular torso. He walked over to Carl, and, as always, the first thing he did was devotedly touch the skin of Carl's scarless face as if it were a talisman. Then, as always, he touched the black hair on Carl's chest and kissed the skin beneath. He let his hand run down the firm stomach to the soft, tender flesh below the beltline. He bent down and licked the flesh. He listened for that involuntary moan before he let his tongue touch Carl's lips. He knew victory when Carl's mouth opened and their warm tongues entwined. He ground his hips into Carl's thick erection, and Carl's arms wrapped themselves around him, willingly, eagerly, and let Ray forget for a while the monster he'd become.

* * * *

Deke was asleep when Hannah slipped away. She wrote a note on hotel paper.

Deke,

Tomorrow night. Same place.

In fifteen minutes, her car pulled up at Bellaire Drive. She entered the dark house and headed straight for the bar. As she mixed herself a drink, a light flicked on in the far corner.

"If you're looking for the gin, you won't find it," Alex told her. "I drank it all. Tonight."

"I don't drink gin," she replied.

She took her drink and walked to her bedroom. She closed her door behind her, glad to be alone. She slid out of her dress and sat in her slip at her three-mirrored vanity. She picked up her brush and idly ran it through her hair as she stared at her mirrored image. She had played it just right, she thought. The only surprise had been how little she'd had to pretend. The surprise had been the unwelcome yearning she'd felt. She hadn't heard the door open, but she saw Moreau's image in her mirror.

"I missed you," he said.

She continued brushing her hair. "I needed some air. I went for a walk."

"In the car?"

"I took a drive. Then I took a walk."

"You should have come to me. I would have gone with you." Moreau came into the room and sat down next to her. He heard the brush moving through her hair. He found the hand in which she held it. He took the brush and gently smoothed her hair with it. Hannah was staring at his face in the mirror when Alex's image slid right above hers, the blind Moreau unawares.

* * * *

Alex stood silent at the door, seething. He watched his father brush this woman's hair as if he were her maid and wagered his murdered mother had never enjoyed such solicitude. And then he saw the image he dreaded—that had scalded itself into his memory. He shrank from mirrors because he knew that specter sat inside them.

Years ago, rummaging through Hannah's things, the young Alex had caught his image in her mirror. He stared deeply at it, and he wondered how different it would be if he were like them. He wondered if, then, he could quell the rage. He wondered if, then, they would look at him; if, then, they would touch him. So he took her puff and dipped it in her white powder and smeared his face with it. A white line formed, erasing a piece of his face. If that puff had been a razor, the cut would not have been so deep. Blood and bone might have oozed where the powder caked. Revulsion twisted him at the sight of what he'd done. Even at his young age, he knew enough to be appalled at the attempt to squelch his very self, and, as if in revenge, he struck himself again and again with that rag, and then he grabbed the lipstick and stained a bright red parody of a mouth on the chalk white face. He stared at the minstrel in the mirror and smiled in bitter hatred at the vengeance he'd wreaked on himself. Then Hannah had entered.

She laughed. Hand over her belly, she covered her mouth and laughed. She laughed harder and louder and pointed as she laughed some more. As Alex's twisted visage watched her laughing in the mirror, something changed inside him.

Chapter Five

Early next morning in the empty restaurant, Barker sat at a table with several decks of cards before him. Expertly, he shuffled them and verified which contained the five queens, the three aces, the four of each suit. Alex had ordered that Deke was to win, and he would.

That afternoon, Pritchett was the first to arrive. He entered the perfectly appointed playing room and let forth an audible sigh. His proximity to beautiful, exotic things moved him. The ornately patterned rugs from the Orient, the mirrorlike sheen on the mahogany table, the sparkling crystal chandelier overhead—they fed the illusion that he was a man of the world, instead of a man of Moreau. Honey and Tate soon joined him. They made a beeline for the drinks, which Jimmy served with his usual disdain.

Deke spent the morning in his room. He'd had his breakfast there and didn't even bother to dress. He thought about last night. Lying on his bed, smoking now and then, stroking his own chest, he thought about how lucky he was.

When he got to the playing field, he realized he'd seen attempts at rooms like this, but even his Texas eyes could tell that this was the real thing—downright coffinish plush and comfort. Too bad they were here to play poker, he thought, and not to die.

When Alex arrived, they all took their seats. The game officially began.

* * * *

Stacy nursed a cup of coffee in the crowded hotel restaurant as the poker game progressed behind closed doors. She awaited a woman. For a man, she would have dressed to welcome his flirtations and inappropriate intimacies. But not for a woman. In with her wide-brimmed hat and high-necked jacket, she sought impenetrability—to assure herself the upper hand.

She smiled when Hannah entered the restaurant with the blue crumbled envelope in her hand. Hannah strode bull-like toward the table, and Stacy knew her missive had had the intended effect.

"Hannah," Stacy greeted.

"What's this?" Hannah threw the crumpled envelope on the table.

"Coffee?"

Hannah just stood there.

"I suggest you sit, dear. You're attracting flies."

Reluctantly, Hannah sat.

"Coffee?" Stacy repeated sweetly.

"No, thank you."

"Carl," Stacy called to the waiter. The handsome young man arrived. "Could you bring Mrs. Moreau some coffee?" Stacy suggestively touched the front of his jacket.

"Yes, ma'am."

"Rough night?" Stacy needled.

Hannah didn't respond. She glanced around the restaurant

as if her mind were a thousand miles away. Stacy took it as another sign of the superior airs Hannah affected and became even more determined to puncture them.

"I thought you and Moreau were early-to-bed types." She had never forgiven Hannah for not being her friend. They should have been. In the same "family," so to speak. But Hannah kept to her house, where she played the high and mighty holier-than-thou common-law whore/wife; and that's why this was so delicious.

"So devoted to one another. You're a regular Florence Nightingale."

"I love my husband," Hannah said absently.

"Step down, girl. You were seen."

Fear touched Hannah's face.

"Right out on the street. At least I have the decency to do it in cars."

"When the gutters are full?" Hannah spat.

"You were right out in the middle of the street, for God's sake. What did you expect? You think everyone's as blind as Moreau? I never figured you for stupid."

Carl returned with the coffee. "Here you are."

"Thank you, Carl," Stacy said.

Hannah stood. "I'm leaving."

"Sit down!" Stacy barked. Hannah didn't move. "Moreau would kill you for this."

"Does Pritchett think it's morning dew all over his car seats!?" Hannah hissed.

Stacy laughed. "Pritchett's harmless. He can't even use harsh *language*. Moreau uses guns, and worse. You've got a pretty face, Hannah. Think what it would be to lose it." Stacy touched her own face. "I don't think I could live like that, could you?"

Hannah's wheels were spinning.

"Sit down," Stacy said.

"How much?" Hannah said as she sat.

"Let's not start with that. I wanna know what's going on."

Hannah lit a cigarette. "Just what it looked like."

"Don't tell me true love struck. Alex invited him here. He's been here two goddamned days."

Hannah stared at Stacy as if studying her, with that cool, distant air that always made Stacy feel sub-par.

"You're a vulgar woman, Stacy. You deserve to be here," Hannah said calmly as if proclaiming the results of her investigation.

Stacy had all the cards, and she could have spat at this bitch for managing to hurt her anyway. "Vulgar, yes," she said a bit sadly. "Stupid, no."

* * * *

The room had filled with smoke. Jackets were shed and ties had loosened. The ashtrays had been filled and emptied many times. Stacy made a habit of dropping in on the game from time to time, standing over Pritchett's shoulder, watching him flub good hands and call when he should have folded. She liked being the only woman in the room. (Honey didn't count anymore.) Forty-five, and still something to see. Forty-five, and the game still stopped when she walked into the room. It had this time, too, as she'd sashayed in and, particularly triumphant, took her place next to her husband. Pritchett felt quite proud of his wife just then.

After meeting with Hannah, she'd had to ponder. She'd been tempted to throw it in Alex's face, to run and whisper the whole sweet deal to Moreau. That's what she would

have done, years ago. But she was older now, more tem-
perate. Took her time. That's what the young men liked
about her, after all. That, she thought, is what keeps them
coming back.

"What do you want, Stacy Pritchett?" she'd asked herself.
"What do you want?"

The heaving had come from nowhere, and the sobs that
followed shocked her, as if blood suddenly poured down from
the sky. She'd looked at her wet fingertips, astonished. She
stood there, in a stall in the ladies room of L'Hotel Moreau,
her arm across her heaving middle and cried like a virgin girl.
"What do you want, Stacy Pritchett?" She kept hearing it over
and over. It's a question she hadn't dared pose for half a life
because she couldn't bear its mootness. She'd given up asking.
Now, suddenly, she wept with a kind of ghastly relief at
hearing it clang as relentlessly as church bells, because she
knew those bells would lead her far away from here.

She took some time to steady herself before she joined the
players in the poker lounge. She dried her eyes and touched
up her makeup. She removed her hat and jacket. It took that
little to transform her woman's outfit into a man's.

"Five card draw, gentlemen," Barker called.

"You're a real pissant, Barker," Honey groused.

"*Lady* and gentlemen," he corrected himself.

"Lady, my ass," Tate tittered.

"Fuck you, Tate."

Drink didn't agree with Barker. His formerly pristine shuf-
fling had grown ragged. Deke had noticed, and so had Alex.
Deke wasn't complaining, though. He held a pair of tens.
Honey, clutching one ace, hoped for a blessing. Deke opened
with a bet of two hundred. Everyone called. Deke took three
cards. Barker hit Deke with another ten, giving him three of a

kind. Honey took four cards, and she got her wish. She now had a pair of aces. Alex took two.

Deke bet another three hundred. This group was easily intimidated. Lay down enough cash, and they scurried like roaches. Honey called, as expected; so did Alex. The surprise was Pritchett's call. When he raised another two hundred, all heartbeats quickened. Tate pulled out. The poor man of the group, he barely made it to the end of any hand.

Alex watched Barker fingering the deck, looking worried. When he caught Alex watching him, he straightened up and silenced his restless fingers.

Honey called and raised another two. Deke called.

"You three should play alone," Alex said as he folded.

At show time, Deke displayed his three of a kind—three tens.

"Shit in my lily-white drawers!" Honey'd been sure she had it. She showed her losing aces.

Pritchett stared at his hand. He held two tens. There were five tens on the table. A Mona Lisa smile played on Stacy's lips as her eyes flew right to Alex.

"It's only money," Pritchett said as he threw his cards on the pile facedown and stared at the visibly frightened Barker.

Deke collected his chips.

"God must be on your side, Deke," Stacy purred at Alex.

"Clean livin'," Deke replied.

"Let's just say we call it a night," Pritchett said. He shot Stacy a look meant to warn her not to go too far.

Honey rose and stretched unattractively. "God damn," she complained. "This fuckin' game better be over. These chairs are pretty but they don't sit worth shit. My back can't take any more."

"Next time I'll order up a toadstool," Alex mumbled.

"What do you plan to do with your winnings, Deke?" Pritchett asked, fishing.

"I've got some plans."

"There must be a woman," Stacy said, with a Cheshire Cat smile to Alex. "There's always a woman behind a man with plans."

Alex didn't even grace her with a glance but, for Stacy, watching him stew was good enough.

Barker hurriedly collected his cards and scurried away. All knew he'd lock himself in his room and feast on his own fingers.

Everyone else packed up and headed into the Mardi Gras night. Alex didn't move. Pritchett also kept his seat.

"What are you up to?" Pritchett asked.

Alex just held up the cards he was toying with.

"I'll find out."

"Too late," Alex said. "You'll find out too late."

Pritchett stood and walked into the empty restaurant, which, in anticipation of a celebration, dripped balloons and colored strings of paper. He heard the sunset revelries beginning outside: the firecrackers and the shouts and the laughter and the bands.

Honey shielded her eyes as she left the building. "A little on the bright side out here, don't you think?" she said to Tate as she blinked at the setting sun. "Maybe Moreau can grease some palms, shorten the days."

"If he could do that, he could grow himself some eyes," Tate guffawed.

"Go on and crack yourself up. Someone hears and you'll be huntin' for that prize dick o' yours."

The two stumbled merrily down the street as Stacy emerged from the hotel. She waited for Pritchett. Tapping her foot, ready to burst with excitement, she was pleasantly surprised that she wanted to share her delight with him.

"Well?" she attacked him the moment he appeared. "What did he say?" He met her eyes, and she felt her joy drowned by the heaviness of him.

"Nothing. He didn't say anything." Pritchett kept walking.

"You know what he's doing. You saw it." Following behind him, Stacy demanded, "What are you gonna *do* about it?"

He turned on her. "NOTHING! I'm going to do *nothing* . . ." And he made "nothing" sound like so much. For the first time she had *something*, a hope, and he dared ennoble the very nothingness she thrilled at sloughing off.

"You look disappointed," he said. "That means you have a hope. What are you up to? What have you got up your sleeve?"

She shook her head dismissively.

"It can't work," he said gently. "Whatever grand plans or grandiose designs. If you'd just accept that there are some things you cannot change, we might be happy. It might bring you some peace. It's brought me my only peace."

She stared blankly at him, eyes full of contempt.

"There's nothing I can do," he said, finally. He could not reach her. She did not love him.

She turned to walk away.

"Where are you going?" he called.

"Someone who *can* do something is waiting for me."

"You paying this one?" He shook his head with priggish distaste. "I don't enjoy the idea of my wife having to pay."

He disgusted her. He should have been a catalogue model for the cuckold's horns. "You're an idiot, Pritchett."

"No, Stacy," he replied. "I am a fool. You: You're the idiot."

As she walked away she could smile at it. Yesterday. Yesterday it would have hurt.

Chapter Six

The early fireworks exploded like confetti in the light blue sky even before the sun had set over the city. Half drunk at the bar of his father's house, Alex prepared himself for the task before him. He was not angry at Stacy's taunts—at the fact that she obviously knew about Deke and Hannah. He was tired. He could see it all before him: the changes of plan, the striking of fear, maybe even the killings of women and men. It would require so much of him. The expenditure of resources would be monumental. The prospect made him tired. Had he been an old-style monk, he would have walked the streets, whip in hand, lashing his own back to the bone. Instead, he dissolved the masks of power, privilege and grandeur that he wore one atop another; and he remembered the fury and loneliness behind his blighted face in Hannah's mirror. He let every hurt he'd ever felt berate him. Every need that he'd denied. He thought of how his mother died and how his father killed her—the blood and the blindness of it. The years he'd spent pacing between this mausoleum and that hotel, all the while playing the best role he found the courage to take—that of the caged, rare animal on display for the black and white folks to gawk at. Seated on his bar stool, he tried to drink enough to kill all his doubt. He tried to drink enough to prepare himself to do what he'd been born to do.

Moreau entered the house with his German shepherd all trussed up like the blind man's tool it was.

"Did Hannah come in alone last night?" he asked.

Alex immediately knew that Hannah was through. His father would not tolerate having to ask such questions about a woman he owned.

"Yeah. She was alone. You smell semen on her breath or something?"

"Shut up!" His father's sense of decorum was quite Old World. He'd butchered more people, Alex thought, more politely than anyone could possibly imagine.

"Of course she came in alone," he corrected himself.

"Where was she?"

"She said she took a walk." He might as well have said that she'd gone cow tipping. He couldn't help but laugh. He took his drink and left the room.

Moreau let go of his dog and sat on the sofa. Then he picked up the phone.

"Tate," he said.

Alex picked up the line in the kitchen and thought he heard a tinge of sadness, maybe resignation, perhaps even (dare he think it?) a soupçon of regret creeping into his father's voice. Yes, Alex thought, it would almost be possible to feel sorry for the man.

"I have a job for you, Tate," Moreau said.

* * * *

Hannah's big silver car glided down the driveway in the dark New Orleans night and headed south, toward the Quarter. A moment later, a pair of headlights flashed on, and Tate's big, flashy car slid silently after her.

Deke heard a roar travel out from the Quarter, as if a testy beast that lay there had been roused from sleep. The first crowds were always the loudest. They went at it the hardest and lasted the longest. Walking to the Ten Spot, as far as he was from the Quarter, he heard the rumble. If he hadn't known, he would have thought a train was rolling by in the distance; but he knew it was just the all-too-human sound of a thousand impenitent appetites.

Deke took the same seat at the same table and waited. Hannah was late. He downed one drink, got scared she wouldn't come, and ordered another before she walked in the door.

From the moment she walked in, he collected images of her—mental snapshots. The way she stood with her outstretched arms leaning against the jukebox; the moment her eyes closed when he laid his palm against her face. He'd forever remember her first laugh, the first honest-to-goodness laugh, since he'd found her again: her eyes scrunched up, her beautiful teeth flashing. The sad, first dance to Horace Silver—"Lonely Woman."

And he'd remember forever that look of hatred, for an instant, before it disappeared behind a smile.

"A few years after I left you," he told her, "maybe I realized I wasn't all I cracked myself up to be, and I started thinkin' about you. I haven't stopped since. I went back and tried to find you . . . But you'd gone." Looking longer and deeper into impenetrable eyes, door after door burst open behind him. He fell back through each—until he landed in the place he'd spent a life regretting.

* * * *

It had been worse than he'd expected, but he wouldn't admit it. He said he hadn't been afraid. He said it so often and with such conviction that he came to believe it. He even took pride in the lie as he told it more and more often, in the hope that it could become his truth and shield him from ever again feeling such shitting, pissing fear, such disgust at what makes men.

When he came home from the war, his mother kept asking him about it.

"What was it like, son?"

"About what you'd expect" is all he'd say.

Before the war, he'd been working in Dallas. He didn't want to go back there. He told himself that a man who felt no fear deserved more than that. But unable to bear the thought of being alone, he returned home to his mother's warmth and resented her more and more for the chink in his armor that his need for her screamed.

His daddy'd taught him to play cards when he was a boy. Deke had played all through the war. Got to the point where most of the guys wouldn't play with him. Deke had a poker face second to none. He could bluff so well that sometimes he forgot himself whether or not he really had a winning hand. Now, he kept himself in money by playing with his mother's boarders. He'd look around the table and wonder which ones she slept with, which ones were her "regulars." His father was right for trying to beat some sense into her. He was right for walking out.

His mother had taken in a young girl to help out around the place. A pretty blonde girl. Hannah was her name. Sixteen years old, she was alone in the world. When she hit town and started asking, someone told her that Eve Watley let rooms. She immediately liked Eve and vice versa. She wasn't shocked when Eve told her that most of the traveling men were boarders, and a few of them were more. And Eve never asked Hannah too many questions—not after the first few queries brought evasions. If the girl didn't want to talk about it, that was okay. Eve knew that in this life, sometimes, things just happen to folks. The girl and the woman both shared and kept their secrets.

There was something in Deke's carriage . . . his air of imperturbability. Hannah thought he had to be as strong as he seemed. She knew that someone that strong could take care of her.

All the boarders liked Hannah and treated her well. Eve had warned them all to do so. The townsfolk liked her, too; so much so that she managed to minimize the taint on Eve Watley's house. Any house that could hold and nurture such innocence, the thinking went, couldn't be all bad. Of course, Deke knew that this was no place for a young girl. He knew there had to be something wrong with her to stay here, like attracting like and all that.

"You wanna go for a walk with me?" she finally asked him, sick of hinting and waiting. When he agreed, she bounced along beside him quite joyfully and gazed at him. She walked along silently. She waited for him to speak, until she couldn't bear his silence any longer.

"Your mama's a really nice lady," she blurted, "takin' me in and all."

Deke studied her. "Doesn't it bother you?"

"What?" she asked.

"What she does," he replied.

She tried to figure whether he knew or not. She didn't want to tell on anyone, but when she saw that he did, she shrugged. "No, it don't bother me. She's a nice lady." Deke walked on.

"Where you been?" she asked. "What places you been to?" She thrilled at the idea of distant places.

"I was in the war."

"Where?"

"The Pacific."

"You prob'ly don't wanna talk about it," she said. "I'm sorry. It must have been hard."

"No," he instantly corrected. "It wasn't so bad. Not for me."

"I never been outta Texas," she said. "But I wanna go. If I was a boy I woulda gladly gone to the war."

Deke told himself he took her places and did things with her because he felt sorry for her. She started taking his arm when they walked down the street. She made him smile. She wanted him to love her. She hung on his every word and worked hard to make him talk to her and tell her things he didn't tell anyone else. He told her about being scared in the war. He said he wanted to go away and make something of himself. He wanted to be somebody. He knew he had it in him. The war had proven that.

"You gonna take me places, when you're somebody?" she asked him, sitting outside at night.

"Where you wanna go?"

She thought about it. "Everywhere," she said. "I wanna go everywhere."

"Then that's where I'll take you," he said, liking the sound of the power it gave him.

When she leaned forward and kissed him, she knew what would happen. She wanted it to happen. She made him take off all of his clothes, even though they were outside, and she took off all of hers. He looked like a little boy when he held her. He held her like a little boy, desperate and hard. She knew from the way he held her that he loved her back.

One of the new boarders saw them. He'd ogled them out in

the field. He'd come to this house on the mistaken information that he could just buy himself some, only to find that this woman picked and chose. And she didn't choose him. That night, all drunk and sloppy, he crept into Hannah's room and slapped his hand over her mouth. He shoved his other hand up her skirt, ripped her panties off and then unzipped his pants. She managed to bite him and screamed bloody murder when he pulled his hand away. He hit her. The whole house barged in to see her there, blood on her mouth, and this man with his thing dangling from his pants, still half stiff. He blabbed that he saw her out in the field with someone. He said he couldn't tell who it was, but it proved she was just a tramp and wanted it. Scared, tears running down her face, she saw Deke and knew that he'd protect her, maybe hold her, wipe her tears away. She looked at Deke who stared her straight in the eye, coldly and accusatorily. Then he turned his back on her and left her there, with all those eyes staring at her, half naked, and the boarder putting his dick back in his pants.

He turned his back on her. All her tears dried up when she saw his back. The other boarders took the man outside and beat him half to death. Watching from her window, she relished every blow. Deke kept to his room. His mother marched in and told him to tell the truth about the girl or get out of her house.

"That little whore" is all he said.

He left the next day, masking with righteous indignation the relief he felt that he had once more dodged the torturous prospect of living and having something to lose. Hannah never saw him again. She never told who she was with out in that field. She sensed he would have wanted her to, so he could revile her for betrayal as well as licentiousness. She would not give him that satisfaction.

In the eyes of the town, Deke's leaving turned her into what he'd longed to think her. Hannah became a pariah, worse than Eve had ever been. "Figures a whore would find a whore," they said. Men grabbed her on the street while passersby laughed as she clawed and fought. The town trash reviled her. In a way, she basked in it, every hurt, every wound. The sting of martyrdom became her revenge. Each insult was proof of Deke's cowardice, of the vileness of what had been done to her and of the man who had done it. With each wound, she took wretched, Pyrrhic solace in the nobility of her silence. It got to be too much when they took it out on Eve. So Hannah packed up all her nothing, and she left that town.

A few years later, Deke came back and heard what had happened. He said he wanted to find her, but Eve refused to tell him where she was. Deke never forgot the disappointment tinged with contempt in his mother's eyes. He left behind some letters. Eve forwarded them on. Around town, Deke heard folks say that Hannah wound up in New Orleans. But somehow, all the cities and all the towns Deke passed through, year after year . . . somehow he never made it to New Orleans.

* * * *

Smoking a cigarette down the street from the Ten Spot, waiting for Deke and Hannah to emerge, Tate wished they'd change the music. They played that slow, dirgy stuff, "Let It Be Me," or that slow jazz. He wanted something with meat on its bones. A rhumba, "Soul Bossa Nova" maybe. Outside in the silent, pitch-black night, he put his palm flat against his stomach and cocked the other arm at a ninety-degree angle as his tiptoes stepped and his hips swayed to the rhythm in his head.

Then his brain and blood splattered. Tate dropped to the ground like the bones had been sucked right out of him. Alex stopped to catch his breath. He'd been holding the big rock aloft too long. His arms trembled. His heart pounded furiously. He'd had to do it, he told himself. He'd come too far and too close to let Tate ruin it all by reporting back to his father. When he was breathing a little easier, he wiped the red-splattered rock in the nearby dirt and threw it as far as he could. Tate's car sat at the corner of Lafayette and S. Peters Streets. It was a long way to drag a corpse, but having no choice, Alex grabbed its hands and heaved. It took every ounce of strength he had to drag Tate's body back to that car.

He loaded the corpse behind the steering wheel. Tate was a big man. He smelled of cigarettes, aftershave and sweat. He was all wrapped around Alex like a limp snake as Alex struggled to maneuver him behind the wheel. Alex's own sweat stung his eyes as he sloshed gasoline on the backseat. Reaching down, he released the car's emergency brake and put it in gear. He pushed to get the big car moving down the empty street. As it rolled, he pulled a match from his pocket, lit it and threw it inside.

Alex watched the flames grow. It was beautiful: Hell's chariot rolling along, flames licking at the night sky like grotesque whores procuring.

He grabbed his gas can and ran back to his own car. He drove away very slowly down S. Peters in the opposite direction. In his rearview mirror he could still see the flames. He was turning the corner when he heard the explosion. He wished he could have seen it.

* * * *

The bar shook. The glasses on the tables, the bottles, everything shook. The few patrons looked at one another, to confirm they'd all felt the same thing. Some of them ran outside. Deke rose and followed; a quick motion signaled Hannah to keep her seat.

When they turned the corner, they saw the fireball.

"There's a man inside," someone called, and several ran toward the car. They removed their jackets and wrapped them around their arms to try to stave off the flames, but it was useless. They couldn't get near the car. Deke stood watching, and then felt Hannah's hand on his arm. Patting it, he acknowledged the pity of what they'd seen and led her away.

* * * *

Hannah dressed as Deke slept. She didn't want to go. The feel of him took her where she needed to be. She wanted to stay and absorb it, drink it, take it with her. She would need it later on when she was alone. Thank God he hadn't changed—his stomach still taut, his thighs big and firm. There was still fine hair on his chest, but it was graying now. That didn't matter. He had changed no more than she. He was now the man he should have been back then, and that made everything just right.

There was so much to do. Her mind raced with it. Deke was essential, a tool and contrivance that happened to be made of warm, rough flesh—flesh that thrilled her when it pressed itself against her and when she felt it up inside her. She pounded on his chest with her fists when he came, to test him, to assure herself of his solidity and strength. He would not disappoint, she'd decided. Not this time.

Once she was dressed, she slipped out of Deke's room and made her way to the stairwell. In the darkness, she couldn't see Ray's black sheath as he watched from the end of the hallway.

Hannah slid out the back of the hotel. She'd parked on

Burgundy Street because she knew Bourbon would be madness. But when she got outside, she was suddenly drowned in a crowd and had to lean and plow her way through. She heard the band in the distance and knew she wanted to get out before it arrived and trapped her. She'd been away from home too long already.

She used her shoulder to budge her way to her car door and open it. She climbed in and shut herself inside; finally she felt safe. Through each window she saw nothing but bodies. She couldn't move. She planted her hand on the horn, but revelers only whooped and shouted at the added excitement. A man with his face painted red looked right into her window and motioned her to roll it down. Tentatively, she did so. He looked as if he had something important to tell her.

"Swingin' party, eh?" he said and flicked his black tongue at her. Then he dropped from sight, as if the ground had swallowed him. Hannah hurriedly rolled the window back up. She touched the gas and inched the car forward. Men and women immediately smacked, kicked and spat on her car. "Leave it there, you crazy bitch," one yelled. Others hopped on it. They slithered around on her hood as they glared at her through her windshield.

Something caught their attention, and they suddenly climbed off and ran up the street. Hannah saw the coffin held aloft and draped in black. The music was right behind. Through all the usual Mardi Gras faces she saw a sea of black and white—black skin, white shirts, black suits, white gloves. A second-line funeral parade marched toward her, colored men carrying the coffin while a ragged band of brass and drum followed, their horns the voices moaning for the loss of the dead. As the crowds followed the dead man's chorus, Hannah slowly pulled her car away from the curb and eased it down the street.

* * * *

Deke woke to the banging on the door. The first thing he saw was the empty place next to him. He eyed the room. No clothes. No handbag. She was gone.

Then he saw the note on the nightstand. "Remember me," it said. For a moment he didn't even hear the progressively louder pounding. He didn't know where she'd gone. He'd sworn he wouldn't let her go like that again.

"Remember me."

Finally the noise cut through. He jumped from the bed and grabbed a robe off the floor. He had his hand on the door-knob. In one of those actions a man can't explain, he stopped himself before he turned it. He went to the chest of drawers and pulled his gun from beneath his worn, frayed shirts.

"Who is it?" he asked.

"Ray. Open it." Deke opened the door a crack. Ray pushed his way in. He scanned the room as if looking for something. He suddenly stopped. "This is ridiculous," he said. "I saw her leave, but I'm looking around to make sure she's gone."

"What do you want?"

"Get out of here," he told Deke.

"What?" Relaxing somewhat, Deke put the gun back on top of the chest.

"Pack. Leave. Do it now. Where's your case, in here?" He went to the closet, pulled out Deke's suitcase and threw it on the bed. "Go on."

Deke didn't move. Half asleep, he still hadn't swallowed Hannah's leaving.

As if he were dealing with an idiot child who had to be shown, Ray pulled some clothes from the closet and threw them at the suitcase.

"What the hell?"

"You're a dead man," Ray said. "They'll kill you."

"Who?"

"Moreau."

"Alex?"

"Alex, Moreau, all of them. I saw her leave here."

The drowning man saw the rope. "You know her? Where is she!?"

Ray saw the naked desperation. "Oh God, no," he said.

Deke grabbed him by the shoulders and shook him. "Where is she!?"

"You're lost," Ray said with a helpless shrug. "You poor slob."

Almost pleading, he asked again, "Where is she?"

Ray pointed at his sheath. "Look what happened to me."

Deke let him go. "What happened?"

"He did this to me. Alex. And you're mixed up with all of 'em."

"What did he do?"

"Burned me. For calling him names. And you're mixed up with all of 'em."

"You work here. You work for him," said Deke, disbelieving.

Ray laughed the laugh of a man who ate his bitterness daily, like a meal. "Of course I work for him. I'm grateful to him. Who else would have me? Who else would hire—and pay well—a monster?"

"Tell me where she is," Deke said, but Ray was no longer listening.

"I know what I am. But to keep going, I have to bury it." Ray looked out the window a moment. "I do a damn good job of it, too," he boasted as he lowered himself onto the bed, his elbows on his knees. He smiled. "I came here . . . I thought I could . . . redeem myself. Save someone. Like hunchbacks in fairy tales." His smile faded. " But I guess we'll have no happy endings here, huh?" After a moment, he stood. "And now, having dug up what I spend my days trying to bury, I must go and do the hard work of interring it again."

He stopped as he passed Deke. "I could tell you. I could tell you everything I know about Hannah and Moreau and Alex—all of them. You probably deserve it, whatever comes. But I can't. I've done some things that make me physically sick to remember. But I'm *not* a monster. Not yet."

"You don't know what you're doing," Ray said as he opened the door.

There's nothing you can do to a man with half a face. So Deke let him go. Not knowing what to make of it, how much was true, what part lies or hysterics, he watched the door shut. He looked at the gun again. He didn't put it back in the drawer.

* * * *

The next morning, a news story had been placed under Hannah's door about an unidentified man who died in a car fire. She slipped on her robe and stole through the house, hunting Alex.

"What is this?" she whispered, waving the newsprint.

"It's Tate," Alex replied from his perch at the bar. "He followed you."

"When?"

"Last night."

"You killed him?"

"No. He died of a broken heart. Not to change the subject or anything," Alex continued, "but why did you tell Stacy?"

Alex terrified her. Looking at him, she marveled at his progression from hurt boy to vicious man. She remembered him as a simple child begging for attention. The colored maids always collected him when he sought it from the white folks in the house, like her or his father. She remembered irritation at his tears. What more could he expect, she always thought. He was damned lucky to live there at all. From hurt little boy to ferocious man.

She mercilessly crushed the thought that her life's progression had been similar.

"Why did you tell her?" Alex repeated.

She thought about lying only for a moment. "She saw me with Deke." She didn't want to admit that Tate had seen her—that Tate had followed her twice. "There was nothing else I could do. She knew something was going on and knew that you were behind it—"

"It's all moved up," he said, cutting her off. He stood and started pacing. "Tonight."

Hannah's eyes widened to perfect circles. "How *can* we?"

He looked at her. "You'll do it."

She sprang back as if struck.

"Don't be coy. You've done it before."

"I can't!" she hissed, appalled.

"You can be as dainty as you like. Use a feather duster for all I care, but you're doing it. Just make sure it's done by ten. Someone will be over to help with any . . . cleaning up."

"What about Deke?"

"I'll keep him busy," Alex told her. "The less you know the better."

Moreau called out from down the hall. "Hannah?"

"Her master's voice," Alex said as he turned to leave.

"Wait!" she called.

Alex did not stop.

"Hannah?" Moreau's voice grew more insistent. She had to go to him. Before she did, though, she ran to the living room and watched Alex's car slide down the drive.

The menacing gray sky spat rain.

* * * *

Without an umbrella, Alex stood before the simple black granite box that held his mother's remains. Wet, it glistened. He saw his rain-streaked reflection in it. She'd begun this. Would she have been thrilled to see her vengeance? He didn't remember her. He'd been too young. But he knew of her. Her relatives had seen to that, before Moreau had killed them or scared them enough to stay away. She had cared for him—that he knew. She had held him in her arms, and that was enough.

As the rain soaked his clothes and ran down his face like tears, Alex stood among the thousand plaques to dead men and asked for his mother's blessings on his work. This was her doing. Not even the grave could stop a hate like hers. It was why she'd made him, to leave behind a piece of herself that Moreau couldn't touch lest he destroy himself in the process. And for the first time, Alex felt resentment stain his devotion, because no child should be burdened with a womb full of hate. But he didn't have the luxury of debating if she had the right. It could lead to hating her; and that couldn't be. From what he could tell, she was the only one who'd ever come close to loving him.

* * * *

"Hello?"

Deke lay on his bed, fully clothed, waiting. He didn't know

for what. He'd been dozing on and off all day. The phone roused him from one of those half-slumbers. He woke up quickly, though. He listened, rapt.

"Where is she?" he asked. He listened a moment more. When he hung up, he grabbed his hat and ran out of the room. He left his gun sitting on top of the bureau. Downstairs, he ran through the courtyard into the crowds outside. They didn't mind the drizzle. Deke looked up and down Bourbon to spy the shortest way out of the fray; he headed up to Dauphine Street. A woman grabbed him around the neck. Her friends cheered her on as she pulled his head down toward her and put her lips on his. He grabbed her arms to pry her off him, but she held on like a child in a fight. He had to throw her to the ground to get rid of her.

When he finally cleared the throngs, he ran to the bus stop at Canal, where he'd first set foot in this town. He flagged down the next bus.

* * * *

Alex had parked his car on S. Peters Street by the Mississippi River Bridge. Once the drizzle had stopped, he put the top down on his yellow convertible. Near the car sat the well-lighted phone booth from which he'd called Deke. Across the rain-slicked street was the columned no-man's-land beneath the bridge. The dirt and gravel underneath was lit up to keep the vagrants out, and the huge concrete pillars gave the place an air of majesty it didn't deserve. All you could hear was the radio.

Alex hadn't heard this one before. After just three notes, he knew he liked it. Bass. Like someone was hunting on it's strings, searching up and down for something he'd have given the world to find; as if he'd gone mad with the looking for it. As fast as you could count: one-two-three . . . one-two-three . . . one-two-three . . . one-two-three . . . A waltz for the insane. Then the horns came in, and in seven notes played a cruel fanfare and dirge all in one, again and again. Although his foot couldn't keep up, Alex sat behind the wheel with his ankle flailing, trying to keep the frenetic time. His head swayed back and forth in half time. Those seven notes, once, twice, then the change on the last note, then another change on the last, resolving, finishing; the coup de grâce to the melody. Band voices shouting out egged on the riot of noise and drove the frenzy higher and higher. Finding the beat, Alex drummed on his steering wheel, eyes closed, mouth open, his feet pumping and his head swaying. The piano came in, and Alex closed his eyes and saw the lights and the bandstand and the black and ivory laid out before him on his dashboard as he pounded out what was now his own fierce, relentless song.

Meanwhile, standing at the front of a bus, Deke craned his neck to stare out at the glassy streets. He couldn't miss his stop. Every street that wasn't his made his flesh crawl. Poydras, Girod, St. Joseph. Every false stop was a punishment. "Where the hell is it?" he mumbled. He almost jumped through the glass door when he finally saw the street sign reading the unpronounceable "Gaiennie." He stood with his nose pressed to the glass and waited for the doors to open, which they didn't do until the bus had stopped completely—a little joke of the driver's, since he usually opened them ten feet before a stop.

Deke flew off the bus. As it tore away, he looked around but saw only pillars beneath an expanse of overpass. If anyone had been there he would have seen them. The place was lit up like a stage, but there was no one on it. Then he heard something and turned toward the sound. A lighted phone booth stood on the other side of the underpass, and in front of it, as far as he could tell, was the outline of a car. As he headed toward it, he heard its engine start. It must have been moving, but he couldn't really see it; it didn't have its headlights on. He heard the engine's gurgly growl. Then he heard music. It had to be coming from the car. He caught a glimpse of its yellow hood as it passed through a pool of light. In one of those tricks the mind plays, the music seemed louder in the moment that the car was illuminated. The music on its radio sounded like swing jazz—happy; and he wanted happy. He strode toward the car as the swing jazz poured out of it.

Inside the car, Alex knew the next tune. It was Mingus. Again, that bass. This time it sounded like it had made up its mind. The horns were vicious now, like barking dogs, warning. He kept his lights off as he drove slowly toward Deke. He listened to the music. He didn't want to rush. He didn't want to take his mind off of it. He'd delay meeting Deke as long as he could. But then the bass hit double time, and he felt his foot pound on the accelerator. He flicked his lights on. The trombones wailed like animals; he cranked the volume to the max and blared the sounds out into the night.

Deke moved faster. The sooner he reached it, the sooner he'd see her. Then the car lights switched on and the music jumped up and he heard the squealing tires join the din as that car came barreling toward him. Two eyes, a chrome mouth and yellow metal skin were flying at him with every-thing the car had. For a moment he kept jogging toward it. He raised his arm to wave to it. And then he knew. It would kill him if it could. He stopped; he stared at the headlights coming closer and closer, faster and faster, the engine whine on a steady climb and the music blaring like stampeding ele-phants. Why would he kill him? What had he done? No.

This wasn't right. So Deke stood there, and the car got so close he could smell it. For an instant, he saw Alex's face behind the windshield, and he'd never seen anything like it. Alex's eyes were closed, and he was bouncing up and down and shaking his head from side to side like he was possessed by the music, as if it hurt—as if its creation, its beats and screams and moans had summoned this incarnation of him; or vice versa. It was like seeing demons, and Deke just stood there, trembling and when the car got within five feet of him, suddenly the brakes slammed and the wheels spun: it turned hard to the right, its big-finned tail swinging out slamming against him like a dinosaur's. He landed with his feet between the spinning wheels; he felt like someone had lit his body on fire. The car never stopped. The tail kept wagging as its rear wheels dug in a few feet from Deke's legs—only seconds before they would have been crushed, Deke dragged them out of the way. The car whooshed forward and still the music played. Deke tried to stand, but he couldn't. His legs wouldn't let him. He felt them; he didn't think they were broken. It was the trembling. Just the trembling. He looked up at the lights glaring down on him. He looked at the huge pillars as the music mocked their stagey majesty and its frantic blats and beats all but spat on his terror and pain. The engine roar started up again, and again he saw the headlights careen back toward him. He raised himself on his arms, and like an enormous, panicked infant, he crawled until the engine grew so loud, and the measured, metered noise so thunderous that he screamed and, pushing himself to his feet, he ran. He darted around a pillar, and the yellow blur raced past him. He heard Alex, or was it the music, someone in the music, shouting and hollering. The brakes slammed on, and a cloud of dust shot up in the air as the car tried both to stop and accelerate backwards at the same time. The tires finally got a grip; and two red taillights sped toward Deke. There was no way anyone could control all that metal flying backwards, and as Alex turned his head, Deke could see him in there, that huge grin on his face and his gritted teeth. Deke didn't want to die, so he ran. He turned and ran, and the red taillights ran after. He didn't look back. He didn't have to. That car came abreast of him, first the finned back of it, and then the backseat, and the front seat, and then Alex looked right at him with his head still bobbing and swaying to all that unbearably loud, cacophonous sound. The car turned hard left. It swung up behind Deke and sent him off in another direction, but Alex kept the wheel turned and herded Deke like he would a steer, until he jerked hard again to the left and threw Deke into the gravel and dust. Deke felt the sharp grit digging through his skin. He tasted the blood in his mouth. He felt his frantic heartbeat in his ears. He's going to kill me, he thought, but he couldn't stand. He couldn't. So he sat there. Tears streamed down his sweat-soaked face, and his mouth hung open in abject terror as he stared at the car up ahead: stopped now, but its engine gunning. Alex's hands flew up and down like drumsticks on the steering wheel before the beast lurched forward again. It bore down on him—his death—and he would meet it helpless and sobbing like a child.

And then Deke heard the tempo begin to slow, and the horns moaned themselves into whispers, and then silence. The engine stopped gunning. The car lights seemed to dim. He heard himself whimper. He scampered, tried to get to his feet. He thought he might escape in the quiet. The music. It had been as much the music as anything.

"This is jazz radio, KJB in Mardi Gras town, and that was something from Charles Mingus called 'Gunslinging Bird.'"

Deke clutched a pillar and hauled himself up. He threw the top half of his body forward and forced his legs to follow.

"That is killer, it's the meanest and I dug it so much on this Carnival night," the DJ announced to the emptiness all around, "that I'm gonna play it one . . . *more* . . . TIME."

Deke heard the howl from the car as he tried to drag his torn body anywhere. He heard the engine again, heard it roaring and roaring, and then he heard the tires spinning out of control and squealing with delight as they sped toward him. He turned around. There it was. He didn't even feel the pain when he flew into the air.

He heard the music, too, when he woke. He turned his face in the dirt and saw a colored man standing on the hood of a car under spotlights in the middle of a theatrically columned nowhere. Deke thought it was the colored man making all the clamor. It had to be him. When the piano came in, he hunched up his shoulders and his fingers splayed to hit the notes just right. The bass entered, and he leaned over, his head low and the fingers of one hand dancing up and down while the other plucked out the sounds. Deke could see the trombone slide shimmer in his hands. And when all the crying and screaming horns blared together he played them all. Then playing the final notes, he slid the bow across the bass like its lover. At the end he leaned back, his arms not quite at his side; sated, spent. The night was silent for a moment, and that seemed sacrilege. There should have been screaming, feet stamping and cheers, hands slapping against one another hard enough to bruise the flesh. But there was nothing. Just Alex, drenched in sweat, having done the impossible for no one.

After a moment, the DJ started talking. Alex collected himself and leaned across the windshield to flick the radio off. He looked at the bloodied, broken Deke, then sat down cross-legged on the hood.

"You like that stuff? It's the music of mortality, you know. It seemed appropriate. I didn't want to kill you. But then again, if you *had* died, it would have been worth it, don't you think? I just wanted to underline the fact that your petty existence is, at best, an arbitrary thing. And I think I've made my point."

Deke tried to spit the blood from his mouth, but it only dribbled down his chin. "Where is she?" he managed to say through his already swollen flesh.

Alex clapped his hands in delight and threw his head back to laugh at the absurdity. "What devotion! And to that. She's barely human. Well, I'd love to tell you so you could rush out and find a white steed. You seem the type who wouldn't play a rescue without one . . . but first things first. Do you read the morning news?"

After a moment, Deke shook his head no.

"Figures. Well, had you read, you'd have seen an item about a car crash and explosion the other night." Alex paused. Deke perked up at that one. "Near a bar. On Lafayette, by the river." Alex smiled at the newfound light in Deke's eyes. "That's right, Amorous, you were there. The dead man was named Tate. You've met him. He worked for my father. He was hired to follow my father's mistress or wife or whatever they call her this week."

Deke lay there frozen in the odd, awkward angle at which he'd propped himself against the pillar—a crime scene's chalk come to life.

"Yeah. You got it, baby. She tell you she was a secretary or somethin'? She's lucky. My father is blind and has sort of retired from life. He doesn't read the papers. But it won't take the cops long to find his name on a list of clients and come asking questions." He looked very sympathetically at Deke. "Now what's my rich, mean daddy gonna think when he finds out that his PI was killed following his mistress and her lover?"

"We were in the bar when it happened," he protested. "People saw us in the bar."

"He doesn't give a damn about Tate. The man was repellent. He was absolutely obsessed with that dick of his. No one in New Orleans would enter a men's room for fear of being smacked in the face with that thing. No. My father hired Tate to find out about you two. He'll kill you for that. And once the cops bring him into it, he'll find out."

Alex rose and crossed the hood of the car, jumped over the windshield and landed in the driver's seat. "He makes a habit of killing his women," he said. "He killed my poor mother. Granted, she did gouge his eyes out first. But you know, he might just consider that less onerous than faithlessness." He started the car. "She can't run. She wouldn't get far. It seems the only thing to do, is for you to help me kill him. And I'm afraid it has to be soon."

Alex gunned the engine and laughed uproariously. The wheels contemptuously kicked dirt and gravel as the car sped away.

"Water," he said.

She brought him some. He took the glass in both his still trembling hands. He tasted the blood now. He looked at her standing there, and later, he would think it had been her look that made him feel filthy and ashamed. Hers was the gleeful, guilty look of a boy who'd got a bug thrashing on the tip of a pin. He felt as tormented as that doomed insect. She took the damp cloth back into the bathroom. He heard the water running.

"What happened?" Stacy asked when she'd returned to dab his face with the cold cloth. She didn't look at him. She concentrated on the cuts, on the nicks and red blotches. If Deke had listened just a little bit harder, he'd have realized that she was asking questions the way you do when you already know the answers.

"I took a fall. I'm all right."

"My ass, you're all right." She treated him in silence. She put her rag down and pulled him forward, to help him out of his jacket, and remove his tie. He watched her go through her ministrations. He couldn't catch her eye.

"Do you know a woman named Hannah?" He closed his eyes, but he felt her sudden stillness.

"Why?" she replied, her hands just as suddenly busy again.

"Do you know her?"

"I know of her." She rose and, returning to the bathroom, tossed the rag inside. She took the glass and poured herself a drink.

"Who is she?" Deke asked.

Stacy's air was one of gravity and concern, with just a grain of fear thrown in for him to nibble on. "What do you have to do with her?" she replied.

Deke opened his eyes. "Please tell me."

Stacy could tell this was real. She could hear it even through his exhaustion. The way he said it. He loved her, and her hatred for Hannah welled up inside her like vomit. Never again would she so enjoy telling the truth.

"She's the mistress of a very wealthy man," she said.

"Alex's father?" Deke asked.

"Alex's father."

Deke tried to lift himself out of the chair. Stacy ran to him and pushed him down. "Listen to me," she said. "Look at me." She turned his head toward her. "I don't know what you're doing or what your connection is, but stay away from them."

She meant it. She could have stopped it outright, told him the whole truth; but instead, she gave him a chance, threw him a rope. She gambled. He could abandon this posture of love for Hannah, and so lend credence to her forlorn cant that there was no such thing anymore, anywhere, because there was no such thing for her. Or, he could run to Hannah, find her, and die for it. She gaped at him like a witch waiting for a potion to bubble.

Believing what she said, Deke slowly raised his hands and lowered his head until the two met, in a gesture of such longing and remorse that a chill went through her.

She turned her back to him to hide the tears of rage in her eyes. "I guess it's a little late for that now," she said. She had managed to turn her victory into defeat. A moment ago, she would have relished the story she had to tell. Now, she knew it wouldn't change a thing in him. He loved Hannah, and he would always love her, no matter what he knew. It would be about her now, about Stacy. It wasn't Hannah's story anymore. Every filthy bit of it would be hers.

"August Moreau is . . . was one of the biggest crooks this town ever saw." She faced the wall and you could tell she was seeing it all: the face of the young Moreau; the image of her own young self. "Practically ran the place. A wild one, too.

He'd go to Honey's whorehouses and nearly tear the joints down. The bitch hated seein' him walk through the door. Wasn't nothin' she could do to keep him out, though."

Her countenance had changed almost as much as her diction. Gone were the full, rounded syllables, and in their stead came this southern lip laziness. Gone was the grand dame of coquettes. She'd no thought in her head but for her words, and for the first time, Deke didn't wonder what contrivances her smile outshined.

"Then he met Alex's mother." At the very mention of the woman, Stacy grew unnerved. Her head whipped around the room. She found what she was looking for and grabbed the half-full pack of cigarettes, took one without asking and used the lighter on the table. She sucked down a mouthful of smoke.

"They say she was from some island or another. He'd always liked nigger women, mostly Creoles, but this was different. He took up with her; and he changed. Did most of his business by proxy. Rarely left the house."

The cigarette calmed her. She stood in a blue haze of swirls and strands of smoke.

"She had Alex for him. No one could believe he let her have him, I mean, acknowledged him, kept him in the house like a real son." Her face curdled at the thought.

"I said something about it. Pritchett almost shit his pants, but I did. You know what Moreau did? He looked at me while I was talking like butterflies were flyin' out my mouth, and then he sorta smiled and raised his finger to his lips in a silent "sssshhhh." He didn't make a sound. That man used to scare the shit outta me.

"Hannah'd been down in Texas. When she came here, she was hangin' 'round with some middleman . . . He worked the streets, generally guns and muscle. She hated his guts. He wore her like a mink coat and a big diamond ring all in one. She was somethin', all right. Like out of a magazine. I don't mind telling you I hated her on sight. She was so pretty it must've hurt. Her man used to say that when she got to thinkin' she was too good for him, he liked to *steal* it from her. You shoulda heard the way he said *steeaal* and licked his lips. He was a piece o' work. She saw her chance here. One night, she went with Moreau. Next day, she shot the gunman."

Stacy didn't notice Deke turn his eyes to her.

"She would have gotten gas if Moreau hadn't taken her in. But his island woman didn't like that. Everyone'd assumed that black, bitch had put some voodoo on him. Only what kinda hoodoo you think Hannah had goin' for her, huh? Most of it between her legs, I bet. Well, Moreau's island woman didn't like it. She administered her own island punishment for that kind of infidelity. She gouged his eyes out with her bare hands." She paused. "They say Alex saw it all. They say the boy was still watching and didn't make a sound when Moreau's dog ripped his mother's throat out."

Deke tried hard not to react. He didn't want Stacy to see it, but even more, he wanted to be impervious. He should have been. This was a test of the mask he'd worn for most of his life. He packed a gun, for God's sake. He couldn't let a little bedtime story rattle him. Oh, but this was another country. They'd torn down the curtains here. The false fronts had rotted and facades had decayed beyond repair. It was as if men here walked around without their skins—just bloody dermis with tangles of bluish, reddish veins clutching them like long-limbed spiders.

In this dark room, covered with dirt and blood, he sat slumped in a chair, while the beautiful woman standing before him stared out the window. They both reminded him of dogs, each waiting for a shot at the next sure thing, the next easy prey.

Stacy put herself back together, reconstituted her various facades, and with a final salute to affectlessness, she rubbed her arms as if she were cold. As if for lack of anything better to do, she made her way to the door. She had her hand on the knob when Deke spoke.

"What do you have to do with them?" he asked.

She turned but her eyes never met his. "My husband is Moreau's lawyer," she said. "They have enough on us, and we have enough on them, to win each other's death in any court. We're bound to one another. For life. Just like Hannah and Moreau . . . me and Pritchett . . . We'll never be free of each other." She looked at him now. "Any of us."

She stood there for a moment and fought the power of what she had hoped to consider a mere performance.

After she opened the door she paused as if struck by a thought. She turned back to Deke. With furrowed brow she said, "Some say that Moreau had brought Hannah there that night to show off. They say that she saw it all, the gouging and the killing . . . that she saw everything."

She paused again, rattling her head as if to shake off the horror of the prospect. She closed the door behind her.

* * * *

Barker's nose twitched. He had a habit of sniffing the air, like a dog. These days it was wiggling like a bloodhound's. Alex was tense. He usually wielded his power with a lusty, vengeful gusto that Barker couldn't help but envy, even if he was colored. Barker chuckled to himself at the thought. Alex had certainly changed him. Several years ago he would have said "nigger" out loud every time. By two years ago, he'd learned to keep it in his head. After what he'd seen Alex do to Ray, by God, he didn't even think it anymore.

Yes, Alex seemed distracted these days. He didn't pay much attention to anything and had stopped bothering to look Barker in the eye. That frightened him the most—looking in those black eyes. You might as well have stared into emptiness, the possibilities, the capabilities of which were endless. Barker had even brought little things to his attention, to raise a spark—little fuckups and incompetencies that should have kindled an appropriately theatrical punishment. But there was nothing. Alex barely glanced at him.

The staff felt it too. He sensed them getting bold, and that could be very, very bad. Alex wouldn't sleep forever. It wasn't even sleep . . . just a form of abstraction. It had started when Watley came. Something was up, Barker knew, and it was big. That excited him, deep down. He found himself with eyes peeled, taking in every facial tic and nuance to try to find the secret. It was like a child's game to him.

Two things changed that. The first was seeing Stacy practically carrying Deke into the hotel, with him looking like he'd just made love to the underside of a moving truck. The second was a phone call from Alex. Alex had never called him before. They saw each other in the hotel and spoke about business. That was all. Getting that call in his home was like letting the wild dogs in through the front door. For a moment he was too breathless to speak.

"You still alive, Barker?" Alex asked after a particularly long pause.

"Yes, sir. What can I do for you, sir?"

"First, stop kissing my ass. It won't help you, and it irritates me."

"Yes, sir."

"Now . . . smile."

Barker actually did. He smiled, his mouth contorted in a sickly leer.

"Stop that. You look ridiculous. I just mean that I have good news. I have some plans for you, Barker. I want you in deeper. I think you're ready for more . . . responsibility."

Luckily, Barker thought, he didn't own much. Two suitcases would carry it all, and he was sure he could slim that down to one.

"There's some special work that I need done."

"Yes, sir," he said as he wondered where he'd go.

"Just don't be surprised if a little more is asked of you, with, of course, an attendant increase in pay."

"Yes, sir."

"You can kiss my ass now, Barker."

"Thank you sir, thank you."

"That was a joke, Barker." Only a moment after the click Barker was on his feet. The suitcase was under the bed. He could put the rest in a box if he didn't want to wait to get another. He'd go to the bus station and check the schedules there. Right now, he didn't care where he went. He just wanted off of Bourbon Street.

* * * *

The phone had rung but he hadn't moved. Now it was ringing again. The only light in the room seeped in from the street lamps. The ring broke the hum of silence that surrounded him like the dark. It was so late, or so early that even on this Mardi Gras night, the street sounds had all but disappeared. The ringing was welcome. Whatever was on the other end of that phone was not. It wasn't the pain that stopped him from answering. Nor was it fear. Surrounded by darkness and silence in a four-walled room, Deke had found his personal oblivion, in which he could bathe as if it were healing waters. The pain, the thump of his heartbeat in his cuts and bruises, electrified his personal atmosphere, charged it with sensations on which he could concentrate. This was a time for stasis.

The phone stopped ringing.

For the first time in his life he didn't think to leave. That's what he generally did the moment a fist or a word smashed through the walls of his perfect cocoon. That way, he didn't have to face his fear of the smell, the stench stinging his nostrils—fear of stepping in it, of slipping and falling face first amidst it, like he had during the war; when he ran, he didn't have to face the fear of winding up covered with the blood and guts of living.

This time, he would not avert his eyes or stand at the edge of the flames and watch the fire from a safe haven. Deke would stand in the blue of it this time. If he was not careful, his flesh would writhe and bubble like any other man's. This was not bravery on his part. It wasn't even a conscious choice. It was just . . .

It was just . . . this time.

Chapter Eight

Alex walked through the house with an unwelcome sense of melancholy. He'd spent most of his life here. It was part of him, no matter how much he loathed it or what horrors he'd witnessed here. Buried within himself he found a wretched tenderness toward it.

He was surprised to realize he would spare it if he could. All his life he'd dreamt of revenge, and finally, with justice at hand, he could have shown mercy. He smiled at that. The ultimate irony, the cosmic injustice of it. Robbed even of the biblically vengeful, orgasmically entertaining aspects of his hard-fought labors. His better nature would be his undoing, he was sure.

Walking from his room to the front door, he saw his father sitting on the sofa, in his ornately patterned robe, that dog at his feet. Tucked in the corner across the room, a television chattered and flashed. The sound was low enough to be audible but not loud enough to command attention. It seemed like his father's brand of soothing music—laugh tracks, pleasant banter, happy endings—a symphony of what, out of necessity or pride or sheer stupidity, he'd forfeited in his life.

He deserved killing, Alex thought. If ever anyone deserved

a long, slow killing, it was August Moreau. Yet, Alex wanted something more. He felt pity for his father just then and allowed himself romantic visions of rapprochement before the dagger struck. Killing him could become the act of a true son, Alex thought, if, just for a moment, August Moreau could be a father to him.

"I went to the cemetery today," Alex said instead of walking out the door.

August Moreau lifted his head and looked toward his son, and as always when he faced him, all of the hell that August had prayed to forget, and dared not, screamed.

* * * *

Deke finally hauled himself out of his chair and walked toward the bathroom. A sharp, rusty spike of pain hobbled him. His right leg gave out and he fell to the floor. Deke sat there a moment, to let the pain die down, to settle into it, before he pushed himself to his feet again. Favoring his right leg, he staggered onward. He flicked the bathroom switch, and the bright light glared off the white tub and tiles. It hurt his eyes after what seemed like the years-long balm of darkness. Leaning on the basin with one hand, he splashed some water on his face. Then he looked in the mirror.

There was a man in there whose actions couldn't predict, whose motives he did not know. A mystery. He felt half sane standing there, his leg screaming, his eyes staring in the mirror at someone he did not yet know. He was like the live soul of a dead man staring at its own corpse.

He cleaned himself up. He was learning to negotiate the swollen ankle. He changed his shirt and brushed the dust off of his pants. He then took the heavy black phone and set it on the table near the chair, which he gratefully sank back into. He picked up the receiver. A room service clerk answered.

"This is Deke Watley," he said. He was ready now. As ready as he'd ever be. "I believe I have a message."

* * * *

Moreau had held all whores in equal contempt. The niggers because they were niggers and because they were whores, and the white ones simply because they were whores. He liked the niggers best. The squaring of his contempt had made his pleasure all the greater. Christine had been different. Honey had told him about the new colored beauty—an island gal. Moreau licked his lips and prepared for new tastes, new sensations. When he walked into her room, one glance and he saw that there was something different about her, none of the vamp or the coquette or any of the other postures with which Honey armed her whores to please the customers. Her fury was palpable, and the thought popped into his mind that he would do nothing less than catch fire if he dared touch her. He didn't for a moment consider forcing her. Something in her very bearing forbade it. Instead, he did the unthinkable.

He'd never been openly reviled like that by anyone, black or white. The sheer audacity of it astounded him. He wanted to know who she was to think so highly of herself. The long and short of it was that in a different vocabulary, she thought herself a queen. That's the conclusion he came to, the terms in which he chose to put it. He'd never understood her explanations of the islands from which she had launched a boat and snuck onto these shores. He'd never understood her explanations of its hierarchies and its religion. The end result was that, to him, she was a queen. The colored skin that could sink her in his eyes to the lowest of humans, also served to raise her up as the most exalted. He could not have conceived of a white woman as queen. Yet he saw this black one so.

Alex walked toward his father. "How old was she when she died?" He knew the answer, but he wanted to probe up the wound. The deeper the wound, the more he would feel for his father.

"I don't know," his father answered. *For a long time, he paid for nothing more than her company. He told her about himself, about the bloody world he had built. She called him an "evil" man. She said it without revulsion, stated it simply, as if remarking on his blue eyes. She was accustomed to evil. Every white face wore it like bloodred lipstick. Moreau was no worse than the others. They all killed and tolerated killing, maimed and cheered maiming. At least he did not boast his own moral perfection as he walked atop piles of black bodies.*

In turn, she let him feel the fire that bitterness had stoked inside her. She made her living on her back. That that was the least offensive option to her—she who had mastered her grandmother's arts and thus knew, *didn't dream or imagine but* knew, *death— incensed her. She wouldn't live the life prescribed for her. She would not be driven to solitude and lunacy on that wretched island by gifts she hadn't asked for. Nor would she live like second-best among people not her betters. She'd first set foot in Florida and found it wanting. She felt nothing there. She could not sense the soul of the place. Oh, there was plenty of blood in its soil and on its sands, but the spirits of those who'd shed it had not been strong enough. They'd left little behind. She was told of New Orleans, and when she arrived, she knew immediately that this would be her home. She tapped into its shame and its glories like a plug into a socket. Here, she knew, she would use her precious self to rise above her own preciousness, to rise above what a black girl was supposed to even dream of being. She deserved this, and she would have it.*

"Why do you keep me here?" Alex asked. "Why *did* you?"

It thrilled him, being with a strength that matched his own. Christine knew she could use his hubris. She knew that through this arrogant white man, she could get what she wanted.

Moreau yearned to flaunt his black queen. He would have taken her out, walked arm-in-arm down Bourbon Street with her, but she wouldn't allow it. She knew better. She kept him at Honey's place, where he soon spent more time than in his own home. He courted her, right inside Honey's whorehouse. They were king and queen there, with every man who mattered in the city of New Orleans paying them court. Christine was his. No one else went near her.

When she got pregnant, she told Moreau she wanted her own house where she could raise her child. He refused. He demanded she move into his house with his child. Fine, she said. She would take his house as her own, but she knew enough to continue walking in and out through the servants' entrance, despite his insistence that she use the front door.

The talk started soon after she moved in. She urged him to lead a quiet life. She told him her stories and coaxed him to tell her his. She taught him games and words in French. As long as they stayed inside that house, she knew, she could make herself a place. So she took her refuge there, and she knew she'd always have the colored parts of town to roam about in when she needed a place to stretch and breathe.

For Moreau, that was not enough. He had built his world, and he wanted it near him. He invited men over—the same men who'd drunk his scotch at Honey's place with colored girls on their laps. They never came. The ones who worked for Moreau and couldn't refuse grew quiet and strained when she entered the room. She knew that there would be more than talk now, that this wouldn't last, so she started hoarding money. Lying, she'd tell him that she needed this and that and then stash away what she could. Eventually she used his name with the black folk to run her own shakedowns, to form "partnerships" and share profits.

The end began when she bore his son. When he acknowledged the black child, and even spoke pridefully of it, the whispers spread about the "nigger-loving Moreau." The white folks' disgust was palpable. Moreau saw it on their faces. The cops stopped saying "thank you" to the underlings. There was no more "Give my best to Mr. Moreau." His pleasures were not so effortlessly acceded to. His wants were not so quickly filled. Finally, Stacy and Pritchett asked him what he expected when he ran around town bragging, in Stacy's delicate phrasing, about his "pickaninny bastard."

Against some he retaliated. Men died. He killed for Christine; and she derided him for it. This was what Christine had feared. Moreau couldn't kill them all. She needed him to be uncontestably a white man, with all the power and privilege that entailed. She couldn't use him unless he were. She also knew that a nigger lover was as powerless as any nigger. Hers was more brutal than any white voice.

She told him what to do: He started marching white girls all over town and set to putting his business and financial dealings to right. He proved once again to anyone with eyes that August Moreau was a white man and demonstrated the damage he could do. He never mentioned Alex in public again.

Christine did her work too well. Eventually, she saw a change in his eyes when he looked at her. He realized what he'd almost been reduced to because of her.

When she had hoarded enough money to buy herself a life, she told him she would take her child and go. He forbade it. He said she belonged to him after all he had sacrificed. She belonged to him, he said, like the dishes and the chairs.

Years passed. He couldn't let her go. Moreau held on to her like lapsed Christians cling to Jesus, for fear of being without— and he *resented her all the while. Christine grew richer and built her own life in that house. Without him knowing how, she had gotten from him exactly what she wanted. It enraged him that she should be content while he still strove to figure out which he hated more: the world, for denying him Christine; Christine, for being black in the world and insisting he remain white in it; or himself, for loving her anyway.*

Five years after he met her, when Alex was four, he brought Hannah to the house, and that was the end. He had never dared bring a woman into the house before. He had been too much in awe of Christine. To do so was his declaration of independence. He was finally putting her in her place and reclaiming his own.

For her part, Christine had borne Moreau's childishness, his sense of ownership and his growing disdain for her son; but she would not share this house. Her house, the one that she had made safe for herself and her son against all odds, the one that fed her ambitions and that had filled her pockets with enough money to ensure her freedom. She had built this nest twig by twig and she would be damned to hell if any man or woman would demolish it. So as he'd hoped it would, the insult burned itself into her. She succumbed to rage, and he was exalted by it. It meant he had finally reached her. He had hurt her.

She told him that Hannah would either leave that house or die in it. Moreau didn't just slap her. He had reached her, and at that moment she became human, not a queen, but a woman, and a nigger, who deserved whatever she got. He slapped her once and then again, and when she fell back against a chair he held her by the throat and kept on slapping her like she were some rag doll whose flopping head he found amusing. When he stood back from her he was as proud of himself as he had ever been in his life. The vanquishing of no foe had been so difficult. He had been so convinced of this woman's power that for years he'd feared thunderbolts and hellfire should he treat her so. Yet he'd done it, and here he stood.

She had only a moment to decide if this was worth dying for. It barely took that long. To wipe the look from his face forever—to prove to him what she was—would be worth it. A smile crossed her lips as she walked toward him almost seductively. He smiled back at her. He'd fuck the bitch now, he thought, like the whore she was, and she would like it. She put her hands to his face as if to caress it and ran her long, red nails along his cheeks. He leered down at her and grabbed her breast. She whispered in his ear that this would be the least of the punishments he'd suffer at her hands.

And then gouged out his eyes. Her nails dug deep into the sockets. He opened his mouth, but no sound came out. He tried to scream not in pain but in abject abhorrence. The merciless malignity of what had happened sucked the breath from his lungs and left him gasping. Finally he fathered the strength to shout, in short, staccato bursts of confounded horror, and then that animal attacked her. Moreau paid no attention to the noises. She didn't make a sound—but the dog's guttural roars filled the room. Objects were breaking and skittering across the floor. Then it fell quiet.

A high-pitched scream shattered the bloody silence. The boy wailed so unnaturally loud, his banshee's shriek heralding doom so ear-splitting, piercing and pure, he might have been possessed. Moreau reached out and tried to grope his way toward the sound, toward his son, but it was everywhere. It surrounded him like bees. Then the servants rushed in, and their moans and wails joined the unholy chorus. One of them slipped and fell in the blood. Moreau passed out.

Moreau had that dog killed, but every one he owned thereafter was trained the same way. He needed a shield against the rages of hell that he now knew walked this earth. He never set foot in that house again. He had it torn to the ground.

"You're her son," Moreau replied. "That's why I've kept you here."

"She was dead. She couldn't hurt you."

Moreau smiled. "She's done more to me dead than she could have ever done alive."

"You're still scared of her, aren't you?"

"You should be too. She's *in* you."

"Let me go," Alex said plainly. "There's no purpose in my staying here. I can't assuage your guilt. You can't punish her through me."

"Look at my eyes," Moreau said, "and tell me if I should feel guilt. After what she did to me, tell me if I should feel any-thing but—"

"Then why do you?"

"Anything but disgust at someone who could do something so repulsive."

Alex laughed. "Yes, and you're a regular campfire girl."

"She knew just what she was doing. To leave her mark on someone like that. I've thought a lot about it. It's worse than branding someone's face. She left me blind to stare at her face until I died. I've done little else for twenty years."

"You should really call someone up and discuss all this. Just let me go."

"What will you use for money?"

"I'll take what's mine."

"You haven't got anything. No one in this town will put a dime in your pocket. You gonna live like the rest of 'em? Like a nigger? With nothing?"

"I'll take what I'm owed."

"You owe *me*. Who else would have let you live like you do?"

"Why!? Why the great favor?"

"You belong here, that's all." He leaned back on the sofa, disengaging himself.

"Let me go."

"*Nothing* is yours," Moreau spat. "You haven't got a home or a color or . . . a people . . . nothing."

"THIS world is mine," Alex shouted. He marched to his father and, leaning over him, resting his hands on the back of the sofa, spoke an inch from his face. "The one I was born into. You showed it to me. How to hate. What it takes to live in HELL."

Moreau squirmed to get some distance. "You remind me of her," he said.

"I *am* like her. Ever think I might go after you?" Alex pushed himself upright.

Moreau got up. "She and I never finished what we started."

Alex bristled at the challenge. "Swords drawn," he replied. "Gauntlet thrown."

"You're all I have," Moreau said as he began to walk away. "You're all she left me with. And there's nothing left to do to me."

"You have always displayed," Alex muttered, "an appalling lack of imagination."

* * * *

The cane made him feel positively distingué. It was the first thing out of the cab when it pulled up near the cold, glistening surface of Lake Pontchartrain. A chilly breeze blew in off the water. After paying the driver, Deke put the cane on the ground and swung his legs out after. Leaning on it, he hoisted himself upright. Room service had brought it to him. If he'd asked for a live baby duck, they probably would have brought that, too. It was a damn fine hotel, once you got past the guns and the dying and the blood.

He walked up the street and turned the corner onto Lakeshore Drive. He'd specifically asked the cabby to drop him on a side street. He wanted to come upon her, to discover her. He wanted to savor that moment when they first caught sight of each other. She was his past, the bridge between who he was and who he was becoming. She was that piss-poor Texas town. She was his irreclaimable youth, his resting place.

Leaning against her car, she ran her hand through her wild blonde hair. The smoke from her cigarette looked like hellfire and a halo. It was all he had hoped.

"Where'll you take me?" she'd asked him.

"Where do you wanna go?"

"Everywhere," she sighed.

"Then that's where I'll take you."

He walked slowly, with a melancholy air, as if toward a memory. He stopped about ten feet from her. He gave her a twitch of the lip that under the circumstances should have passed for a smile. There were decades of hurt and want all over her, smeared across her face and body, yet she was remarkably and innocently beautiful.

"I am sorry," she said.

"Are you all right?"

"I'm fine," she replied. "Alex wouldn't hurt me. He can't. You?"

Deke lifted his arms in a "look at me" gesture. "Alex ain't shy."

"I'm sorry," she repeated.

"It was all set up, my meeting you here accidentally . . . Wasn't it?"

She turned and started walking, as if she'd simply walk away. "Alex went through my things," she said. She stared at the ground as she turned back and retraced her steps like a little girl putting her feet in exactly the same spots. "He found your letters, the ones you wrote after you'd left me. The ones I never answered."

That hatred again. He'd seen it in her eyes in the bar where they'd met. Pain shot through his ankle. It wasn't broken, just sprained, but it hurt like hell. That look of hers hurt worse. Her eyes blazed at him when she said "after you'd left me." She almost spat the words through clenched teeth, and with such foolish, weather-beaten pride she'd announced she never answered them. He so longed to do right by her.

"He asked me if I wanted to see you again," she said, still looking at him. "I said no." Again she beamed with pride. "But then he kept pressing it," she said. "And I kept remembering."

Slowly, her face retreated behind its veil of indifference. "Finally . . ." And all the fight was gone. Like an old phonograph winding down, she just faded into silence. "Finally, I said yes."

The breeze kicked up again. It felt good. They both let it wash over them.

"I didn't know you'd be there that night." She said it with such guilelessness that he had to believe her. He stopped himself from limping over to her, with his cuts and bruises and cane, to hold her. Her craven need practically dragged him there. When she looked in his eyes he knew that the hate and the longing and the want . . . all of it was real.

"They say you killed a man," he said.

"Just like you," she shot back. "I had my reasons."

They stood silent. "What are we gonna do?" he asked.

"You've got to go," she said. She moved quickly for her car.

He rushed toward her. He looked like a cartoon Quasimodo as he contorted his body to keep the weight off his tattered ligaments. He managed to grab her arm before she slipped in the car.

"If I leave, they'll kill you."

"Stay, and they'll kill us both." She yanked her arm free, sank into the car and started it.

"Remember me," she said.

The car sped away. Stranded, alone in the empty street, again not knowing what to do or the next step to take, he watched the car disappear. Then he started hobbling toward the rising sun. He didn't know what his next step would be. He tried not to think about it. Something, he was sure, would come up.

Chapter Nine

Stacy left her hotel suite dressed in her Catholic schoolgirl best—high-necked white blouse, blue skirt with a matching jacket, discreet blue and white pumps. Her small hat had a veil, which she did not lower for fear of appearing too . . . melodramatic.

A bonfire blazed in the middle of Bourbon Street. She eyed it briefly, but its incongruity and potential for mayhem were dwarfed by the magnitude of her mission. Tonight she was delivering the most important news of her life, and she wanted everything to be just right. She feared she might be jumping the gun—not all the plans were completely laid or the details set—but she *felt* that the time was now.

Immaculate, Stacy slid into her Cadillac, and when she closed the door with a solid *thunk*, her whole world retreated behind her. As if inviolate in an airtight bubble, she traveled down Bourbon Street, the fiery no-man's-land between the insult of her past and the glorious future she had arranged for herself. She felt proud that she could leave with no regrets. After all, she had gotten what she wanted. She had married Pritchett to get rich, and he had made her that. Young, though, she had assumed that power came with money. It hadn't, and thus she had spent her life sharing with Pritchett his luxuriant servitude. That he tolerated it sickened her. That she shared in it sickened her more. Had he been more of a man, she thought as she parked her car and walked through the perfectly manicured Garden District courtyard—had he been more of a man, she would not have had to face the fact of her own cowardice.

"What do you want?" Pritchett said as soon as she entered his house—her house. She closed the door behind her. He lounged idly on the sofa, a drink in his hand. The radio was playing Johnny Mathis, "Chances Are"—sentimental garbage as hollow as the man listening. Stacy eyed the Polynesian teak, the bowls from China, the Indian bronze. Rich leathers and elaborate brocades bespoke a world that no longer existed, as imagined by a man who had never been there.

Pritchett noticed that she looked good, younger even. He was half drunk, and he didn't want her here. He needed all his wits to deal with Stacy. It made him even angrier to see her, unwelcome as she was, looking well.

"I want to say good-bye," she said.

Pritchett burst out laughing and took a big swig from his drink.

"You can't go anywhere," he said.

"Let's do this right, huh?"

He realized she was serious. He stopped laughing.

"I . . . *August* won't let you go," he corrected himself.

"He can't do anything to stop me."

He put his drink down and leaned forward. "What are you up to?" he asked, his curiousity redoubled, as if it were a game she'd share with him.

"I can't do it anymore, Pritchett." As always, the onset of emotion astonished her, as if she considered herself biologically incapable of feeling. Her eyes glistened. She fought the urge to let the tears run down her face.

"What, Stacy? What can't you do?"

"Live like this."

"This is good. You live well."

"You know what I mean," she said.

And he did. The cynicism simply masked his fear. He had married her as a bulwark against the ugliness of this life. When he discovered she couldn't make his imprisonment feel like freedom, make the blood taste like wine, he had simply let her go and allowed the gales of her lusts and dissatisfactions to toss her where they would.

"We don't have to live like this," he said. He was a little surprised, and even exhilarated, to hear that come out of his mouth.

If she had only asked "how," he just might have found a way. Nothing would have ever been the same.

"We don't know anything else," she said.

It felt good to Pritchett for that moment, the puffed-up feeling that came with wanting something and feeling for an instant that he could have it. And then, as if dropped from a height, he was back on his sofa, a glass full of memories in his hand, a sentimental song on the radio.

"Do you know that I still love you?" he asked her.

The old Stacy would have mocked him, but this one considered his question, the answer to which was a cold, hollow "yes"; and those tears finally fell, because it should have meant more.

"I guess we just got old here," she said with as good a smile as she could muster.

"Do you know what you're doing?" Pritchett asked. "What are you doing?"

"I'm leaving here."

With that, she turned to the door. As she opened it, she heard the words.

"I'll take you."

She paused for a moment. Those words were the greatest kindness he had ever shown her. She clutched them tightly as she closed the door behind her.

Pritchett poured himself another drink to rinse the seemingly permanent taste of failure from his mouth. He stared at her photograph on the bookshelf across the room. It was taken soon after their marriage, when she could still pretend. In it she had her arms around his neck and the look on her face was one of sheer adoration.

The radio continued playing sentimental songs. "Maybe if I pray every night / You'll come back to me...Ohhh, maybe." He poured himself another tall one from the bottle on the table. Hating her just a little more than he hated himself, he picked up the phone.

"It's Pritchett," he said. "Let me talk to August."

* * * *

Moreau fingered the hands of the clock as a servant answered the knock at the door. The clock read 8:55 p.m.

"We'd like to speak to Mr. Moreau."

"It's rather late," the servant replied.

"It's all right," Moreau called out, rising from his seat. After Pritchett's call, he expected surprises.

The servant opened the door and the two suited men walked in. Moreau approached them.

"I'm Detective Taylor, and this is Detective Simms. We're sorry to disturb you, sir."

"Please sit down, gentleman. Can I get you anything?"

"No, thank you," the first detective said.

"Just make sure it's done by ten."

Hannah heard the voices. She walked softly down the hallway. Keeping herself out of sight, she listened. Fear didn't begin to describe what she was feeling. It was as if she was leaping into a chasm. She knew a soft landing awaited her, but she couldn't ignore sight of jagged rocks as far as the eye could see. She shivered at the thought of what she had to do.

After nervous looks at his younger partner, the first detective cleared his throat and reluctantly did his duty.

"Sir, a man who used to work for you, Harry Tate . . . He was killed last night."

"What was that name again?"

"His name was Tate, sir. Harry Tate, a former private investigator. He worked at your hotel."

Moreau put a thoughtful look on his face. "Yes. I remember him now. I'm sorry to hear this."

"Do you know any reason why someone would want him dead?"

"Oh, no. I haven't dealt personally with Mr. Tate in . . . over a year."

"Hannah?"

She jumped at hearing her name. It was as if Moreau could see through walls and knew she'd been standing there.

"My wife will be very grieved to hear this."

After a moment, Hannah walked in the room. The officers stood and nodded their greetings.

"These gentlemen are police officers," Moreau said to her. "They tell me that Tate was killed last night. They were wondering if we knew of any . . . enemies, motives?"

Hannah pitched her voice low to keep it under control. "That's very sad news," she said, surprised that her voice did not quaver. "But I'm afraid I only knew Mr. Tate slightly."

"I'm sorry we can't help you, gentlemen." Moreau rose from his seat, an indication that the interview was over. Hannah smiled, nodded and disappeared down the hallway. The second detective looked quizzically at the first.

"But I believe we have a few more . . ."

"Thank you very much, Mr. Moreau," the first detective said.

"If I can be of any help," Moreau added, "don't hesitate to contact me. My servant will see you out."

The servant dutifully appeared and the detectives followed him to the door. Moreau heard the door close amidst mumbled good nights. The servant returned.

"Will you be needing anything else tonight, sir?

"No, thank you."

"Good night, sir."

"Good night."

The light switch flicked. Moreau stood in his element—the dark. He wondered if moonlight was pouring in through the windows. He used to like the moonlight. He followed Hannah's path down the hall.

He heard a rustling when he reached her doorway. She was pulling off her dress and putting on her dressing gown. She sat down before the big, round mirror of the vanity, which had two smaller round mirrors on the sides, and began brushing her hair. In all three mirrors she watched the image of three Moreau's staring down at her.

"I had Tate follow you last night," he said.

"And I thought you trusted me."

"I don't trust anyone." He walked toward her.

"What did he tell you?" she asked.

"Nothing. He was obviously killed before he could report." Right behind her now, he put his hands on her shoulders. "You don't know anything about his death?"

"I've never been unfaithful to you while I've lived in this house. I owe you too much for that."

He let his hands slide down her strong shoulders. He touched her hair.

"Is it still blonde?" he asked.

"Yes."

Christine used to read a bedtime poem to Alex. Though the boy loved it, Moreau had never understood reading such a grisly thing to a child. The way she read it, though, with such an ache and understanding, turned the gruesome act it described into one of undying love. Moreau had always remembered the words. He spoke them now.

> *That moment she was mine, mine, fair,*
> *Perfectly pure and good: I found*
> *A thing to do, and all her hair*
> *In one long yellow string I wound*
> *Three times her throat around*
> *And strangled her. No pain felt she,*
> *I am quite sure she felt no pain.*

The rocks of that precipice grinned invitingly at Hannah. She stood. She turned to face him. His hands touched her face.

"Are you still beautiful?" he asked. He loosened her gown and it fell. He lightly touched her soft, smooth skin. He put his hand to her chest and felt her heart violently beating. He touched her breasts, caressed their contours, traced the rise of her nipple, then slid down to the soft mound of her belly. "I do love you," he said as he slipped his hand between her legs and kissed her hungrily. She quivered when his finger slid inside her. His erection dug into her flesh. She clawed his robe off him; she pulled up the white T-shirt and exposed the graying hair on his still powerful chest. She rubbed her hands across it as he lifted his arms and threw the shirt over his head. He took her in his arms now and, crushing her body against his, he filled her mouth with his tongue while his hand slipped down to her vagina and with his fingers forced a shudder from her.

He unzipped his pants and pulled his stiff penis free. He pushed down on her shoulders until her mouth surrounded it. He threw his head back and moaned when the head of his shaft met the back of her throat and caused her to gag just a little. She unfastened his pants and pulled them down; she wrapped her hands around his buttocks and, squeezing them tight, dug her nails into them.

He drew her up by the shoulders. Kissing her hard, he guided her back to the bed. They fell on it. He kicked his slippers off his feet; he tried in vain to slide the pants from around his ankles. He pushed her legs apart and thrust himself inside her. She looked him in the face: the two dark circles of his blind man's glasses bobbed emptily above her. Then she did what she had never done. She pulled the glasses from his face. The eyelids sat concave against the two empty sockets. Small scars from the stitching dotted the skin beneath each eye. The monstrousness made it easier. She reached behind her head and found the handle of the hunting knife she'd hidden beneath her pillow. But at the same moment she tried to get her hand around it, a steel vice clamped shut on her throat. Strangling her, the muscles in his neck bulging with the force he exerted upon her, he kept pounding himself inside her. She pulled at his arms, but she couldn't move them at all. She thrashed at him but her fists were as ineffectual as gnats against him. She couldn't breathe. He liked it. The more she squeezed her thighs around him to hurt or deter him, the more he liked it. Not even those expressionless gashes that had been his eyes could hide the pleasure he felt. A buzzing grew in her head. Again reaching back beneath the pillow, she struggled to get hold of the knife. The blade sliced into her fingers as she groped for the handle. She hoped only to stay conscious long enough to get a grip on it. She felt dizzy. She barely knew Moreau was inside her; she felt submerged beneath it all. She scarcely registered that she'd taken the knife by the hilt. She raised it up, but she hadn't the strength to thrust it down, and so it fell with her hand, as she prepared to die.

She gasped, she choked; her attempt to draw breath suddenly succeeded. Her head cleared. She saw Moreau's back arch, his face twist. And then she saw the blood on her hands. His body jerked spasmodically as he came inside her. Whimpering desperately, she yanked the knife out of him, then jabbed it back down into him, then wrenched it up and thrust it in again, and again, because she couldn't believe she was really doing Moreau harm. He was immortal. Any minute she knew he'd grab her throat again and this time simply snap it.

Spent, she lay still. As she calmed, she felt the blood seeping onto her. It felt warm and good. Moreau lay where he had fallen—on top of her. Blood poured off each side of his back. She simply breathed. She was not yet convinced that she was still alive and that she would remain so; she could not yet believe that even deathly still and gushing blood, Moreau would not rise up again. She gingerly pushed at the body and got no response. She waited. She pushed at it again. Nothing. Only then did she begin to believe he would never cause her pain again, never threaten her again, never frighten her again.

She had won.

Her head fell back, and only half of Moreau's head fell into in her field of vision. Mostly, she stared at the blank ceiling. She did not move. A calm swaddled her. Lying there, soaking in a dead man's blood beneath a dead man's body, she discovered effortlessness. Placidity. Emptiness. She lay there as if she had no bones or muscle; no mind, no heart. Just flesh.

* * * *

After he got the call, Ray had prepared himself for anything. No amount of blood or bile could have shocked him. He'd worn an old raincoat that he could discard after the work. But this, this . . . this scene he walked in on, this was something beyond . . . something truly . . . *macabre*. He smiled. Leave it to Alex, he thought. Alex had said he'd "misplaced" Barker. Ray had assumed that the little man was dead, or else was fast approaching unrecognizability. Ray had been told there might be a mess, but this looked instead like a painting from another age: two nudes, a beautiful woman and a man lying on top of her, both of them utterly still; the blood red against the white sheets and their white skin. The man's attitude screamed death. The arms' awkward angles and one leg's unnatural line told the tale. His mouth hung open and limp, and the one visible eye looked as if a flap of flesh had been soldered over it. Though as immobile as the man was, the woman seemed very much alive. The man's body rose and fell with her breathing; her eyes open, she was staring up at the ceiling, as if she'd lain down to rest completely unaware of the blood-drenched corpse lying on top of her. Dim light from a vanity lamp lit the pair to morbid, gothic perfection.

The woman's eyes turned toward him. She woke from her stupor. She squirmed a bit under the dead man's weight. She began to slide herself from under him. She didn't say a word. Standing in the doorway, Ray watched as she pushed at the big man with her bloody hands and finally got one foot on the ground, and then the other, so she could scoot from beneath him. Ray watched her naked, blood-spattered body emerge. It transfixed him. Her implacability, her utter indifference, mesmerized him. Then she looked back at him. A chill went through him, and the smell of blood made him gag. He barely knew Hannah. She was with Moreau, so she was out of the running for sainthood—that he knew—but those were not a woman's eyes that looked at him. They belonged to some better, wilder creature. He did not move beneath that gaze. Then she walked toward the bathroom.

Ray shook his head to clear it. He knew what to do. He went to Moreau's body and pulled the pants up the legs as far as he could. Turning the body over, he was surprised at how heavy it was. With all his strength he lifted and shoved to get the pants back up around the man's waist. He saw the T-shirt lying near the bed, but went to the closet and chose a buttoned shirt. He then lifted the corpse at the waist and fought with it the way one would with a reluctant child until he'd slid the shirt up its arms. The scene was almost comic.

His raincoat looked like the smock of an artist obsessed with red, but he had gotten the corpse dressed again. Already, the buttoned shirt was soaked with Moreau's blood, and the jacket Ray had placed over it was now beginning to seep with the viscous stuff.

Ray stood back, like a butcher with an aesthete within. Panting, beads of sweat on his brow, he surveyed his work. The large, bloody knife lay on the bed beside the corpse. It would do better in the body, Ray thought, with his usual foresight. He hesitated, though. The prospect was gruesome even if this was a corpse. It was gruesome even in this butcher shop. But then he looked down at his blood-splattered self; his hands, thick with the stuff, were drying to a dull reddish-brown. There was something liberating in the bath of blood. What the hell, he thought. It wouldn't hurt him to strike a blow at the man who'd started it all, the man who bore the ultimate responsibility for the whole damned mess—for Alex, Hannah, him . . . all of it, all of it come together here, tonight, in this charnelhouse crescendo to Moreau's masterwork. There were certainly simpler ways to die, he thought; but it was a measure of the man that he gruesomely embraced all his children in his own bloodily rococo denouement.

Ray pulled a piece of plastic from his pocket and picked up the knife. Grabbing the handle with both hands, he jabbed the knife through the flesh so that the bloody handle stood up tall and straight. It startled him how little resistance the flesh offered.

Clean and dressed, Hannah returned from the bathroom. Without a word Ray glanced at her and walked past her to the bathroom. She'd been as thorough as he. *It's been a pleasure working with you*, he thought. There wasn't the slightest hint of red in the sparkling white room. Washing his hands, he stared up from the reddish water swirling against the white porcelain.

Up to this point, his thoughts had been cynically jovial. The farcical aspects of the whole affair were too glaring to ignore. *"Everyone, please take a firm hold of your corpse, and lift . . ."* Then he got a look at himself in the mirror. His black sheath covered almost half his face and allowed just a bit of the scarred tissue around the eye and neck to show. Moreau's blood was smeared all the way up to the collar of his raincoat. Not just a monster now, but a bloody monster playing patty-cake with corpses. He remembered having been a man.

He looked back down at the sink. Rinsing it thoroughly, he left it as spotless as he had found it. Hannah was putting on her jewelry when Ray emerged. He went straight to the corpse and, grabbing it from behind, under the arms, prepared to drag it out to the waiting car. Just as the legs hit the floor with a thud, a low growl stopped him. In the doorway Moreau's huge German shepherd, its hair up, stood snarling at him. He froze.

"Caesar!" Hannah's voice rang savagely. She snapped her fingers and pointed to a corner of the room. With the snarl still on its lips, the dog skulked toward the corner, where it reluctantly sat. She was not human, Ray decided; she was no less a monster than he, he thought, as he dragged the corpse across the room. Just better looking.

Chapter Ten

Frenzy reigned on Bourbon Street. Barrel fires burned, and the bodies cavorting around them seemed as rapt as lewd priests at dead men's pyres. Deke couldn't take three steps without some drunk man or woman slamming into him. He was the only one on the street not ricocheting wildly with a rapacious smirk on his face or his private lusts smeared, draped, painted and sequined all over his body. Kids set off firecrackers that sounded like guns. Men and women screamed at the noise.

He didn't even know why he was out here. He felt he should be. He supposed it was where he belonged. This was what the world had come to—fire, madness, like something out of hell. He had to walk among the embers. He passed a derelict mumbling to himself in a doorway. A man helped a crying woman inside a building. Her dress was torn and bloody.

"Nice to see you, slob."

A hand grabbed his shoulder. Deke turned. At first he didn't recognize Alex in the dashing caballero outfit and matching sequined mask. With a flourish, Alex flung his cape over his shoulder. Deke turned away.

"Now, where you goin'? We're partners, remember? We

have things to talk about." Alex grabbed him and hauled him out of the center of the fray.

"I'm leaving tomorrow," said Deke, freeing his arm.

"That's most unfortunate. We could've had such fun together. Oh, and with the money you could have won here, you and your lovely Hannah could have enjoyed a life of bourgeois bliss. Poor Hannah."

Alex slipped off his mask. "It's not your neck, so I guess it doesn't matter. But it is hers. I'll see to that. I might have already seen to it." He dove back into the crowd.

"Wait!" Deke stared into the drove, but it was useless. He couldn't see him. Deke was again left waiting for the fates to guide him forward. He had figured Alex would have been good for a sign, but surprisingly, he'd gotten nothing.

"Good-bye, little man. Go home now." The voice came from above. Deke jumped further out into the street. He looked up. On a second story balcony stood Alex.

"Go home now," he said as he whirled around and disappeared.

By the time Deke reached the hotel, red and blue lights were smashing intermittently against anything in their path. Police cars, at least five of them, sat outside. A gawking crowd filled the courtyard. Deke pushed his way through. Still fastening her robe, Stacy marched toward him.

"Come with me." She dug her nails into his arm and dragged him through the crowd to her doorway.

Once inside she slammed the door and hissed, "It's your room!" and marched toward a desk in the corner.

He stared out the window. "Is it Hannah?"

"*Moreau!*" They found Moreau's dead body in your room."

For the second time, he made a friend of terror—that noxious cocktail of confusion and whimpering helplessness. At the desk, Stacy scribbled on a piece of paper. Deke looked expectantly around him, as if answers could be found in the very air. Through the bedroom door he saw a young man lying on Stacy's bed. Deke recognized him from the restaurant.

"Did you hear me?" she said as she opened a desk drawer. "There's a rich, dead man in your room. You're wanted for *murder!*"

"I wasn't there. I didn't kill anyone."

From the drawer Stacy pulled a loaded .38 and a box of bullets. She ran across the room and piled the note and the gun and the bullets in Deke's hands.

"This is a place I know. Go there. Hannah will meet you there." She looked out her door and peered around the corner. "It's safe."

Deke stood slack-jawed and stared at the red lights circling the world outside.

"GO!" she yelled. She pushed him out the door and slammed it shut behind him. He almost banged on her door to let him back inside, but a hundred eyes were ready to turn on him.

He slipped the gun in his pocket. He lowered his head. Slipping sideways and muttering "excuse me," he began easing his way through the crowd. As he opened the gate, he looked up through the yucca plants at his second-story balcony. Jimmy stood there looking down. Deke could have sworn he saw a smile cross his face.

"There he is! There he is!" Jimmy shouted.

The crowd screamed and scattered. Deke ran. A gunshot almost shattered his eardrums. Another shot exploded. The pain ripped him wide open; it slammed him into the gate. Amazed at the dazzling intensity of the fire inside him, he stumbled forward. The carnival crowd swarmed ahead, and he lumbered straight for it. Warm blood dribbled through the fingers he held to his side.

He slowed down when he reached the thick of the crowd. The cops were pushing through. The pain burned his flesh from the inside. He rode the crowd to the intersection, where he turned off onto Conti and headed south. He ducked into an alley and collapsed against a heap of trash. He let the pain crawl all over him. He didn't look at the wound; he didn't want to. It was less real if he didn't see his own insides.

Footsteps came around the corner. By the sound he knew one set was a woman's.

"Please, help me," he said. He reached out his hand to the approaching couple.

"He's bleeding," she said.

"He's just drunk," the man replied. "Come on." They walked away.

Deke tried to stand. He couldn't. His legs felt too weak to support him. The pain was excruciating. He leaned against a wall, then pushed himself to his feet. He leaned forward and let the momentum carry him.

Toward the end of the alley he heard voices.

"Tommy, stop it," said a young girl.

"You ever seen one before?" a boy asked.

"My little brother's."

"No. I mean a big one. A man's."

Deke felt something on his foot. A huge rat was picking at the blood that had trickled down his leg. Gasping, he kicked madly at the filthy thing. His foot hit a trash can and set off a metallic din, and pain savaged his side.

The boy's shirt was open and the girl's blouse undone to expose her brassiere. Crouched behind some boxes, they jumped to their feet when they saw Deke's bloody form lurch up in front of them.

"We ain't doin' nothing, mister," said the boy, holding up

his hands. Deke realized he was holding the gun. He didn't recall fishing it from his pocket. The girl hurriedly buttoned her blouse.

"We're goin' right now," the boy assured him. He picked up a mask from beside him; a black cape rested on his shoulders.

"That costume. The mask. Give 'em here."

The pair inched away; they scooted along the edge of the alley as if on a narrow beam. "We're goin' now, mister," the boy repeated.

"No. No." Deke lifted the gun. The pair froze. "Go ahead. Untie it."

The boy undid the knot at his neck and threw the cape at Deke's feet. He put his hands back in the air.

"And the mask."

The boy threw the mask on the cape.

"Go now. GO!"

They ran. Deke managed to get the cape around his shoulders. That would hide the blood.

He emerged from the alley onto Bienville. There were fewer people here. The pain in his side had become a constant, a sustained shriek, a kettle whistle of pain instead of the shouts and hollers he'd had before. He pulled Stacy's piece of paper out of his pocket and studied the directions: Rampart Street. He had to cross Bourbon again. He hoped that with the costume, it would be safer. He donned the mask and headed back.

The minute he hit Bourbon he saw two cops scanning the crowds. They walked right toward him, but he kept his pace. A man and two women had their arms around each other. They swigged from a bottle as they sang and danced their way along. Deke threw his good arm around one of them. He planted a big grin on his face despite his agony and sang along with them. They handed him the bottle and, putting their arms around him, welcomed him to their merry band. One of the cops strode right past them. Deke took a huge gulp from the bottle, and then another. The liquor spilled down his chin. One of the women grabbed the cop.

"Hey, love," she said. "You wanna dance with me?" She looped her arms around the cop's neck and planted a big, wet kiss on his lips. He didn't push her away. Finally, peeling her arms from around his neck, he walked on to continue the search for the man who stood right beside him. Once across the street, Deke slipped down another alley.

He was heading in the right direction now. He found Rampart and maneuvered the smaller crowds on Toulouse and S. Peter streets. Once he hit Dumaine, it grew quieter. He let himself stumble and lean, as he'd been desperate to do.

When he got to Gov. Nicholls Street, he saw a fat man leaning against a big black Buick as if waiting for someone. Deke straightened himself up and headed for him.

"Hey, mister," Deke called as he passed. "You're leakin' an awful lotta gas back there."

"What?"

"Gas. You musta put a hole in your tank." Deke doubled back and looked in through the window. The key was dangling from the ignition.

The man furiously spat brown tobacco juice and marched to the back of his car. His face grew red, and his countenance suddenly filled with rage.

"Goddammit. I told those sons o' bitches to fix this fuckin' thing. This car ain't been nothin' but trouble since I got it. I swear I'm gonna junk this heap o' shit and get me a Ford . . ."

Quietly, Deke opened the car door and slipped in behind the wheel.

"I don't see nothin' back here," the man said.

Deke turned the key in the ignition, but the car just whined. The man rushed to the driver's door. Deke slammed and locked it.

"Get your ass outta my car. I'll kill you. Goddammit, I'll kill you!" The man pounded on the windshield and yanked at the doors.

Deke turned the key again. Still nothing. The man looked down the street and in the distance saw a set of headlights turn the corner. Deke saw them, too. It looked like a police car. The man ran toward it.

"POLICE! POLICE!" His belly bounced up and down as he ran, and he was waving his arms in the air as if he could grab the cops by trying hard enough. Lights flicked on in nearby buildings.

Deke pumped the gas pedal. "Shut up," he mumbled. "Shut up . . . shut up . . . shut up . . ."

"POLICE!!!"

The car fired. Deke floored it. The car roared forward and the headlights caught the man's jiggling form as he ran down the middle of the street. Deke aimed at the man as if he, of all the threats, had to be eliminated—as if this little fat man's cater-wauling was to blame for every ounce of his hurt and fear and pain. The man turned to see his own car hurtling at him. He slowed, then stopped and just stood there, his mouth open, his arms slowly creeping above his head as if that act of submission could stop the tons of metal careening toward him. With a loud crack the car struck him. It bent him like a doll and flung him into the air. Deke covered his eyes and slammed on the brakes as the body crashed down on the windshield in an explosion of glass. Then it slipped down onto the pavement. The screeching brakes echoed off the buildings; the man's screams hung in the air. Lights flicked on all around. People appeared on doorsteps and stood silhouetted in the lighted windows. Sirens approached.

Deke stared at the bloodied pile of flesh in the beam of his headlights. His heart was pounding. He slammed his foot on the accelerator. The tires howled as he sped away.

* * * *

The police had come and gone. They'd given her the tragic news. Her husband had been killed. She had cupped her hands and dropped her beautiful, tear-stained face slowly into them. It was a heartbreaking scene. Her alibi was airtight, and so her grief was that much more convincing.

And now, seated at her vanity, she brushed her hair, while watching herself in the mirror, as she so often did. Partly adoring, partly dispassionate, mostly afraid, she tried to read the mystery of her very own face.

A dot of blood stained the vanity's white lace. She stared at the blood as she drew the brush through her hair.

* * * *

In the middle of Bourbon Street, the man in the goat's head costume twirled around and around with his arms outstretched and his head cast up at the stars. His crazy laughter stopped only long enough to bring the bottle to his lips. Pritchett planned to drink forever. Mardi Gras would last forever.

* * * *

As if to mock him, the sounds of Mardi Gras stole through his closed, shuttered windows. A once-handsome man with a ruined face sat in the dark—waiting.

Chapter Eleven

Alex wondered who owned the Ten Spot now. Did his father still own it? Or did he? It didn't matter. On this celebratory night, there'd be no trouble. Black folks could drink here during Mardi Gras. He sat at the long bar next to a very pretty, young, brown-skinned girl whose friends occupied a table nearby. In their schoolgirl costumes, they adeptly employed the "hide in plain sight" rule of Mardi Gras debauchery. The girl at the bar kept glancing at her friends. They giggled and gossiped behind their hands while she stifled giggles and swiveled on her stool. Alex watched her, supremely amused.

"This is an occasion," he said. "It calls for champagne." He pounded on the bar. "Champagne!"

"My nuns would have a fit if they saw me now," the girl said.

"Ignore your nuns. They can't see you. Anyway, they preach their chastity, but do you think they practice it?"

The bartender opened the champagne and poured two glasses.

"Noooooooo," Alex said. He raised his glass. "A toast. To success." The girl raised her glass. She dissolved into giggles and glanced at her friends several times before she even got it to her lips.

"Success," she finally said, and drained her glass in a single draught. A high pitched squeal escaped from her friends. She slapped the glass on the bar and covered her mouth with her hands, her eyes ablaze with mock mortification before she dissolved into yet more giggles.

"At night they sneak into rectories, with all those horny Papist priests," Alex continued.

"No!" The barkeep filled her glass again.

"Yes," Alex replied. "They don't turn on any lights, because neither nun nor priest wants to look into the face of a sinner. Those nuns sneak in, and under the cover of night, what do you think they do?"

The girl stared, her mouth agape. Her eyes widened. Looking about conspiratorially, Alex leaned toward her.

"They suck . . ."

Her hands covered her ears.

"Priests . . ."

She stamped her feet in anticipation.

"COCKS!"

"Aaaaaaaaaaaaahhhhhhh hah hah hah." She almost flew off her chair in explosions of laughter.

Jimmy entered the bar. He saw Alex and gestured that he wanted a word in private.

"No. No. Come here. Have some wine. Join us."

Hesitantly, Jimmy walked over.

"This is my good friend . . ." He pointed at the girl and waved his hand decorously.

"Elizabeth," she said.

"Elizabeth," he repeated. "This is my business associate, Jimmy."

"How do you do?" she said, then belched, and collapsed in a fit of giggles.

Alex was quickly tiring of her. He turned to Jimmy. "Oh, Jimmy. Why the long face? Drink and forget. By now our friend is safely arrested, and the police are beating him black and blue to extract a legal confession."

"I need to talk to you alone."

Alex shrugged.

"Where you goin'?" Elizabeth whined.

"I'll be right back."

Jimmy led Alex outside. "He got away," he said.

Alex stared at him as if still awaiting the news.

"He got away. The cops were there, like you said. They went after him, but he got away."

Alex grabbed him by the lapels, his face an inch from Jimmy's. "You let him GO!!?"

"It was like you said. He was downstairs, but he didn't come up. I was watching for him. He didn't come in. He ran. He must have been warned. He talked to Mrs. Pritchett."

Alex let go of him. Pacing, he took a few steps. "Stacy. Hannah. Where's Hannah?"

Jimmy shook his head. He didn't know. Alex paced up and down.

"The ladies," he said. "The dear little ladies." He charged at Jimmy and grabbed him by fistfuls of shirt front. "I should kill you. I should kill you right now. But I'm in a good mood. You find him do you hear me? You find him or you die."

Alex pushed him away. Terrified, Jimmy stood frozen.

"FIND HIM!"

Jimmy bolted. Alex stormed to his car as Elizabeth sashayed out of the bar. Her coquette's smile went suddenly south.

"Hey, where you going? You comin' back?"

Alex ignored her. He jumped into his convertible, made a

violent turn and sped away with the car's rear end obscured in a storm of dust.

He drove like a madman through deserted streets. Rocking back and forth in the driver's seat, he pounded out his rhythm on the steering wheel.

"Oh, Hannah. Die, Hannah."

The car screeched to a stop at Moreau's house. There were no lights. Ready to attack whomever he found, Alex ran through the front door.

"Hannah. Hannah! Heeere HannahHannahHannah . . ."

He stalked down the hall to the bedrooms. Hers was immaculate. Running from one to the next, he checked every room. He found no one. Furious, imploding with unspent rage, he returned to the living room. He knew she'd done it. The filthy bitch. Her picture sat on the fireplace. Alex picked it up with both hands and smashed it against the corner of the mantle. He threw the remains in the fire and watched them burn. He grabbed a magazine from a table, rolled it up, and lit it. With his makeshift torch he lit the bedclothes in Hannah's room. He flung the closet open and set her blouses and dresses and skirts aflame. Then he lit the delicate white silk that covered her precious vanity. He stood back as the fire ate everything that had been hers. Drunk on rage and fire, he ripped the heavy curtains from the living room windows, dragged them across the room and heaved them into the still smoldering fireplace. He torched anything flammable and then stood witness as fire overwhelmed the place. He was breathless and uncharacteristically disheveled. The flames almost caught him. He shielded his face as he tore himself away from the strangely, soothingly cathartic sight.

He'd spent his rage. Watching the fire eat what had been his life—all the taint and all the atrocities—could have been enough. He could have walked away, everything else being equal. But everything was not. He had to claim the spoils of this war, because he would never have another chance in his colored life to gain them. He was trapped. For all his planning, all his time and all his work, he still remained trapped, this time in another drama, a drama not of his own making, but one that he had to play to its inevitable end. He had underestimated Hannah. He hadn't even considered Stacy. He would pay for those oversights. And this time, his opponents performed with all their senses.

He walked out the door; left the house to burn. He rounded his car, and there, by the driver's side, stood Moreau's dog. It glared at him with a fixed, stalking eye. He stopped. It growled and bared its lethal teeth. Alex backed toward the open garage as he blindly waved his arm around behind him. He never took his eyes off the dog. Finally, his hand met a wooden handle. He didn't care what it was. He just grabbed it and thrust it out in front of him. It was an iron rake. He smiled. His luck was turning. It could have been a mop. He held out the business end and, poking and stabbing at the dog, forced it back. It snapped and growled, desperate to strike. "Like mother like son," Alex had said to his father. The old bastard was probably already in hell pulling this animal's strings.

Once past the car door, Alex hurled the rake at the dog, jumped inside, and slammed the door behind him. The dog attacked. Snarling and drooling, it bit at the glass as if it would eat its way through. Alex sat in the car and stared at it. The beast's fury mesmerized him. It lunged and bit in a frenzy of mindless hate. Its nails made an incongruously dainty tapping noise against the glass.

He admired its intensity. He shifted the car into reverse. The dog was still snarling and barking, but it slipped from view. He backed up until the dog reappeared in his headlights. He stopped. In the pool of light it spewed its rage against the impregnable machine. Alex punched the gas. The car struck, and a quick, high-pitched yelp was the only protest. Alex drove on, crushing the body beneath his wheels. Then he threw the car in reverse, backed up over the dog's corpse and stopped. For the millionth time, he relived the scene: the blood streaming like a waterfall down his mother's chest, the dog's white teeth gorily red. He sped forward, the car jiggling like an amusement park ride. Then he backed up and shot forward again, and again he savored the quick, ragged undulation each time the car rolled over what had killed her. He backed up one more time, and this time he drove away.

* * * *

Deke was dizzy when he turned into the driveway of the house that Stacy told him about—the house on Rampart.

Stumbling through the gate and under a vine-covered archway, he almost choked on the lusciously overbearing smell of honeysuckle. The white clapboard main house sat at the end of a long sidewalk. Several steps led up to a generous covered porch. There, the requisite swinging seat hung invitingly. To the right squatted a long, rectangular shotgun house. A curtain parted, and a colored face looked out at him. After a mere glance, the woman dropped the curtain with such disdain, such "just some white man" contempt, that it reminded him just how little business he had being here in Alex Moreau's little world of wonders.

He limped up the walkway. His labored steps thundered on the wooden porch floorboards. He'd assumed he'd been heard well before he turned the knob and entered. It seemed like no one was there. The house was dark. Moonlight backlit the elaborate white lace curtains covering the windows, which threw spiderlike shadows on the walls. At least there were no guns blazing, no tires screaming. All things considered, he was as safe as he was likely to get; he sighed and fell into the first large chair he saw. Leaning his head back, he let the sweat and the fever engulf him.

Hannah entered the room like a wraith. This house was her element, like a vampire's lair or a ghost's ancestral haunt. Her footfalls were silent here, so effortlessly did they mesh with the hums and vibrations of the place. This grandmotherly collection of old walnut furniture with little brass handles, overstuffed chairs and cream-colored lace doilies might well have conjured her. She stared down at the bleeding man in the chair as if he were some newly discovered flaw in this perfect world. As she moved, Deke sensed someone in the dark. Through the mists of his stupor, he fumbled for his gun.

"It's me," Hannah said. "It's me." She put her hands on his shoulders to settle him. She could see his blood-drenched shirt beneath his jacket. She pulled the shirttail from his pants to inspect the wound. The bullet had penetrated the flesh above the hip. It had probably gone straight through. She left the room and returned with some towels. She sponged the blood away.

"I told you to leave," she said, concentrating on the blood. "I don't think there's a bullet."

His head lolled back and forth against the back of the chair. He grimaced at her every touch. "I can't believe I found you here."

"You've got to go. I can give you money."

"Come with me."

She didn't respond. On her knees she poured alcohol on a

clean towel and pressed it to the wound. Deke moaned from the pain.

"You didn't have to kill him," she said as she unraveled the bandages.

"Who?" he asked.

"Moreau . . ."

"I didn't kill anyone," he said. Then he remembered . . . the sirens and the blood and the fat man falling. "I didn't kill Moreau."

"Did Alex promise you something? Was it money? I would have given you money."

"Listen to me!" he said. "I didn't do it! Someone put him in my room."

She continued her bandaging as if she hadn't heard him. He grabbed her by the hair and forced her to look at him. "Listen to me!" he hissed at her. She jerked her head away. He relaxed as she continued rolling the bandage over his wound.

"Alex," she said.

Deke shook his head in assent. "He'll try to pin it on us. What are we gonna do?"

Finished, Hannah stood. "Us? WE!? You got yourself into this. All you had to do was run, like I told you." She stalked off into another room. Deke hauled himself out of the chair. The bandage was tight, but the wound felt better. He limped in the direction Hannah had gone and found her in a bedroom as ornate and Victorian as the living room. She was pulling men's clothes from the closet. Deke rested against the doorjamb. Again he felt the car shudder as it threw the man's body in the air; again he saw the lifeless heap of limbs smash into the windshield.

"I might have killed a man back there."

The quick glance was her only sign of surprise.

"I pulled a gun on a couple o' kids to get their costume."

"These ought to fit you," she said, fumbling through clothes, unfazed.

"Is this how it started with you?"

That fleeting hatred he'd seen in her eyes flared up like wings. "GET OUT!!"

Amazed, he just stood there.

"GET OUT! I hope they KILL you!" she shouted.

Her face twisted into a mask of hate, she charged at him. She pummeled him with her fists while a child's desperate tears poured down her face. He tried to fend her off, but he was too weak, and her blows threw him to his knees. He found his feet and stumbled through the doorway and back to the living room. He turned, and there she was, still slashing at him. He leaned back against a table and managed to push her to the ground. She lay there, breathing as if the air were too thin, her hair about her in a medusan crown.

"I . . . WAS . . . GOOD!" she screamed. "I was PRETTY! They ALL said so!"

The room spun. A violent movement and everything changed—as if someone had pulled the conjuror's tablecloth trick—pulled the world out from under him—and Deke was the china left teetering.

"Oh, God," he said. "Oh, God."

* * * *

Stacy's oriental robe barely covering her nude body, she lay on her bed with Carl. He was naked. They giggled mercilessly. There was a bottle. They'd drained most of the liquor out of it. Half-packed suitcases sat strewn about the room.

"Tomorrow we'll be gone," she told Carl. "Go on. Call."

He shook his pretty head. "No . . . no," he said with a smile that insisted he could be persuaded. Stacy laughed at his transparency.

"Can you imagine the look on his face, or what's left of it?" They both laughed helplessly.

Carl looked at her and bit his lower lip. "All right," he said. Hunching up his shoulders in naughty anticipation, he reached for the phone. While he dialed the number, Stacy crawled all over him, up the silky hair on his chest, down his stomach, around to the sharp curve of his buttocks. She purred and cooed.

"Sshhh!" Laughingly, he pushed her hands away.

"Hello, Ray? This is Carl." Stacy covered her mouth for fear of erupting in audible guffaws.

"Listen, I can't make it tonight."

Stacy buried her head in a pillow, her body shaking with mirth.

Carl's voice quivered with his own amusement. "I have some friends coming in from out of town." There was a pause. Carl shrugged at what must have been the silence on the other end of the line.

"So I'll see you tomorrow, all right?" Carl concluded.

He listened anticipatorily for another moment, and then put the receiver back in the cradle. He and Stacy looked at one another, but the expected convulsion of laughter never came. In its place, with a dismissive flick of the head, Stacy kissed him drunkenly. She pulled open her robe and ran her hands up his firm, fine-haired torso. She climbed on top of him and felt his thick erection grow between their bodies.

* * * *

"Fine. Tomorrow," Ray had replied. He sat in his desk chair, near the phone, where he'd been waiting. Ray continued sitting there. It seemed the thing to do. He imagined himself a portrait . . . *Man in Darkened Room with Mask* . . . and then, quite suddenly, self-pity wracked his bones. His head snapped back; his mouth opened wide as if to scream. He constricted himself in a fetal position. His fists clenched so tightly they trembled. His whole body shook, as if cold.

And then, just as suddenly, his anguish passed. Slowly, he unclenched his fists. He let his arms fall to his sides and his feet touch the ground. He breathed again, and with that breath, he knew he had been cleansed.

* * * *

Like a dime-store novel gumshoe Alex stepped through the bushes and fought the spines of yucca plants to get to Stacy's window. He'd seen the lights on. Now he had to know if she was there. He had to know if Hannah was with her. Through a partly opened window—Stacy had assumed the dense foliage would satisfy any debts to modesty—Alex saw her astride some boy. He saw no sign of Hannah. Were she there, he doubted Stacy would have taken her eyes off her long enough to violate the child.

By the time Alex hacked his way out of the bushes he looked like he'd been attacked by a swarm of needles. He tingled all over from the spiny plants' poison. It was Ray's friend he'd seen under Stacy. Yes, he decided; he would have a talk with Ray.

He climbed the hotel stairs instead of taking the elevator. The effortlessness of mechanical elevation didn't suit his mood. He knocked softly on Ray's door, but he got no response. He knocked a little louder, again with no response, so he pulled his passkey and went on in. He passed through the empty living room and found Ray in a chair in the nearly dark bedroom. The downright beatific wisp of a smile on his face made him look like the Mona Lisa with a skin condition.

"You look contented," Alex said.

"You look like hell," Ray replied.

Alex scanned himself in a mirror to survey the damage, which was extensive. "Had to do a little trailblazing." Ray continued to stare into space with that silly grin on his mouth.

"There's been a mishap."

"Yeah," Ray smiled. "I heard he got away."

"You didn't have anything to do with that, did you, Ray?"

"No."

"Then it must have been Hannah and Stacy."

"Then he's off to a far worse hell than we're in," Ray said. His blood-splattered image in Hannah's mirror flashed in his mind.

Alex located the bottles and poured himself some gin. "I was just down at Stacy's," he said. "She's celebrating her triumph . . ."—he took a long draught—"smearing fetid juice from that twat of hers all over Carl."

Ray's smile disappeared for only a moment, then sprouted again, now even more serene, with just the hint of a quiescent "oh, well" thrown in.

"She's been sniffing around him for a long time. I've heard her giggling about it. She's the one who warned Deke about the setup, probably thinking I'd blame you. You are the one with the biggest grudge to bear. God knows what she thought I'd do to you. She's quite something, our Stacy." Alex finished off his drink. He watched Ray's every blink and twitch. "I'll have to do something about her," he said.

"There's no need," Ray replied. He looked up at Alex, who understood. Alex set his glass down and left Ray alone.

After a moment, Ray picked up the phone. "Room service," he said.

Chapter Twelve

An irritated Stacy answered the knock at her door. The bellboy wheeled in a cart carrying a beautifully arranged tray with a glass pot full of coffee, a perfect rose in a delicate crystal vase, and a bone china service for two.

"I didn't order this," Stacy said.

"It was ordered for you, ma'am."

"Who ordered it?

"I don't know, ma'am."

She puzzled over it for a moment as the hop wheeled the cart in, then she shrugged and let it go.

* * * *

Ray pulled a pearl-handled .22 caliber pistol from his desk drawer. It had been a gift from an old lover he'd abandoned after his . . . accident. Ray missed him. They had laughed and fought and called each other pet names. He had written saying he didn't care about Ray's face. Ray had destroyed that letter, and the next and every subsequent one, until they stopped coming.

Standing before the bathroom mirror, he took a good, long look at himself. He might have thought the face of a handsome man hid beneath the black mask. He lifted his hands and undid the thin strings that tied the sheath around his forehead, then undid those around his neck. The mask fell.

With a passkey he let himself into Stacy's rooms. He'd never been inside before. He turned the burner to maximum underneath the coffee pot. He gawked at the artistic pornography on her walls—paintings filled with pink, dimpled women's flesh and satyrs' bulging muscles. A statue of Michelangelo's *David* sat on a table. He walked to the bedroom. Carl lay asleep on the bed, while Stacy, sitting up next to him, nursed a drink. She glanced at Ray, and only for a moment did her eyes widen in horror. Though she quickly mastered her revulsion, the blood had already drained from her face. She couldn't control that. Sensing dissonance, Carl crawled out of his stupor and opened his eyes. He gasped audibly, and shrank back. He pulled the sheet up over his naked body and began inching off the bed.

"Get out of here," Ray said to him. Stacy sipped from her drink.

"She told me to—" he began to protest.

"GO ON!"

Carl grabbed some clothes from the floor as he ran. Stacy tucked her left breast back into her robe and cinched it up tight.

"What do you want?" she said into her drink.

"Look at me, Stacy." She seemed completely transfixed by the thick brown liquid.

"Look at me."

She took a moment, but then raised her head and looked. He turned the ravaged side of his face toward her.

"How do you like it? Pretty, huh?"

"If you came here to disgust me," she drawled, "you've succeeded. You can go now." She swung her legs off the bed and pulled a cigarette from the pack on the nightstand. She lit it, then picked up her drink and walked right past him into the living room. Ray followed her.

"I don't have very much," he said. "Couldn't you have done it to someone you wouldn't take . . . *everything* from?"

Her eyes betrayed guilt and shame that even her bravado couldn't cover. "It's more fun that way," she boasted. "I like my fun." She sipped her drink and smiled.

"Oh, I would have loved to see the look on that nigger bastard's face. I just wished I'd been there to see him put in his place. Hannah and I did pretty well, don't you think? She and Alex use Deke to get rid of Moreau, I help her use Deke to get rid of Alex, and we stroll off two rich women of the world." She tried to look at him. She couldn't do it, though. Her eyes couldn't light on that face.

"You should be enjoying this as much as me," she said, "after what he did to you."

"Where are they?" Ray asked.

She shrugged as if it didn't matter at this point. "The old house on Rampart," she said. "The one that belonged to that nigger witch of Moreau's."

Ray looked in the bedroom. "He was here, when he called me?"

She barely shook her head.

"I could hear you laughing." He pulled the .22 from his pocket.

"You expect to kill someone with that?" Stacy sneered as she turned to refill her drink.

"No."

Bubbles danced around the edge of the coffee pot. Ray picked it up. When Stacy turned to meet his gaze, the heavy glass shattered against the bones in her face and the boiling liquid transfigured her skin. Her screams even pierced clamorous Mardi Gras night. In their visceral horror, the unthinkable pain they knelled, they were unlike anything else to be heard. Ray watched her shaking hands unable to touch the fiery flesh. The pain was too great for that. Her eyes shined brightly, disbelieving, as her mouth howled useless, foghorn-like protestations of agony and incredulity. He remembered his own screams of not so long ago.

He tossed his pearl-handled .22 toward her before he left the room.

* * * *

Like an idle tourist, Alex sat in the hotel lobby reading a newspaper. His dirty, charred clothing and the dots of blood on his face and hands shocked no one. People invariably assumed he was dressed for the Mardi Gras.

Ray approached him in the lobby. Ray spoke to him in whispers. The disheveled, blood-specked colored man listened intently to the tall white one with the mask covering half his face. They cut an odd figure. Alex never said a word. He just watched Ray's impassive features and marked his tone—as soothing and studied as a mortician's informing the family that the blotches on the corpse's face were merely the first signs of decomposition. Nothing to be concerned about. When Ray had finished, Alex shook his head in appropriate, though feigned, gestures of bewilderment and acceptance. Ray turned and walked away, and Alex watched him get swallowed up by the red, writhing walls of that hotel. Alex could spot a broken man when he saw one. He'd never known Ray very well. He hoped that he had never been a good man. That would have been sad.

* * * *

The phone rang. Deke and Hannah both stared at it. It rang again.

"Answer it, Hannah," Deke said. "It's the last hand. Might as well play."

They still staged their eloquent tableau: he, thrown on the sofa nursing his pain; she on the floor in her black, sleeveless cocktail dress, recovering from a wrenching bout of tears. As she rose, Deke saw that her visage had regained its steel. She regarded him coldly, then pulled herself fully upright and walked to the phone.

"Hello?"

"Hello, Hannah," Alex's voice answered. Hannah nodded to Deke.

"Alex," she said.

"Deke there?" Alex sat behind the desk in the hotel office, the brass desk lamp the only light, like any man of business working late.

Forgetting his pain, Deke pulled himself off the sofa and rushed to Hannah's side. He turned the phone so he could hear.

"Does he know?" Alex asked. "You were the fall guy, slob," he said more loudly, as if the truth had to be yelled to reach anyone it might do some good. "It was all her idea. You want *me* now, huh, Hannah? That's what this is all about."

She stared at Deke and knew he could believe it, and because of that her hatred for Deke grew all the more monstrous.

"Leave us alone!" she howled into the phone.

"That's not what you want, Hannah." Sitting on the desk, Alex felt tired. All the weariness he'd fought for so long settled down on him. "You couldn't stop now if you tried." That was the truth; and it meant that he could not stop either. Not enough people were dead yet.

Her look dared Deke to believe what he heard. Her eyes

burrowed into him and in him deposited every hurt he'd caused her, every kindness and all the love of hers he'd squandered; and she dared him to believe it.

"Where will we meet you?" she asked. Deke moved away from the phone while Hannah listened a moment, then cradled the phone back on its hook. She looked through the lace curtains out into the moonlight.

"You might as well rest," she told him. "We've got some time."

Those were the most welcome words he'd heard. He lumbered toward the bedroom. A few moments later, Hannah followed and saw that he had passed out on the bed. She returned to the living room.

"Get me the police," she said quietly into the phone.

* * * *

Stacy mastered enough of herself to claw her way to her feet. Her warped image in a picture frame's glass told her everything she needed to know. It was over. She had lost. She had bet her life, and lost. The twisted image was like the royal flush slapped down on the table. Losing this much should have meant more. She was surprised at the mere . . . disappointment—the head tilted to the side and the long, sad "awwwww" of it. Was it good sportsmanship on her part? Had she made the wager and come prepared to pay the price? Atta girl, she thought. A good loser. Good at *something*. How could she have got it so wrong? She had gotten everything wrong. Her sobs almost turned to laughter. Her face. She'd been killed. She stood there, the pain startling every nerve in her body. Absolutely nothing left. It was funny really. The irony was overwhelming. She laughed. Who'd have thought that the nigger and the queer could have done this to her. She laughed and laughed. Stacy loses. The shame of it. Her pride couldn't take it. Like dying on the toilet or choking on her own vomit. There it was, on her face. She picked up the gun because she couldn't stand the brand on her—what it meant, having it scream that she was a loser. She couldn't look at that. In a movement as swift as a slap she swept the gun to her head and pulled the trigger. At least now she wasn't a loser anymore.

Chapter Thirteen

The place had an air of threatening romance about it. Like old dolls and weathered clowns, the sinister had infested it and warped its innocence. He had parked a block away, and then walked. He was carrying big wire cutters. With them, he cut the chain locking the six-foot gate at the Pontchartrain Amusement Park. He closed the gate behind him. Inside, he marveled at the empty midway and its skeletal outlines of Ferris wheels and arcade booths, merry-go-rounds and barkers' stands. This was a dead world. It had ended, if only for the night, until the next morning when the crowds arrived to people it again. For now it was his. All his.

He dashed off into a shed no bigger than a closet. He examined the dials in the moonlight and pulled one of the levers. Outside, a merry-go-round lit up like a Christmas treat. Its red, gold, and blue lights ripped brightly colored holes in the darkness. With the flick of another switch, a wax gypsy fortune-teller popped out of the dark; for a dime she'd tell your fortune. Up and down the midway, orange-haired clowns prepared to chuckle, multicolored lights blinked and flickered, haunted houses groaned while tiny trains awaited tiny passengers. Alex backed out of the little closet and gawked at the feast of color and light. This was his private Mardi Gras, his personal carnival of dead things and innocence.

He dashed to the merry-go-round. Circling the perimeter he hunted for the controls. He found them and pulled the lever back. Calliope music jangled and the shiny, stationary horses began bobbing slowly up and down. He jumped on the spinning platform and climbed aboard a particularly sparkling stallion, its mane flying and its head held high in a wild, triumphal silent whinny. He reveled in the breeze as the world whirled by him like a dream.

* * * *

Rumors raged that a madman had done it. Sirens screamed. Hotel guests shook their heads and covered their mouths as they craned to get a glimpse of the mutilated corpse. Ray fled the shocked onslaught of pink chiffon nighties, striped pajamas and fur-trimmed slippers. He retired to the closed-up restaurant, grabbed himself a bottle, and pulled an upturned chair from one of the tables. He nursed his third drink and the magical stuff began to cast its spell. He didn't hear Pritchett approach from behind.

"She killed herself?" Pritchett said, half a question, half statement.

"I can't tell you how many times I've thought of it," Ray replied. He didn't look up from the table. He slurred his words.

"I loved her," he said.

"She did not love you."

"Stacy didn't love anyone. Most of the time she couldn't stand Stacy."

Ray downed the rest of his drink and poured himself another. "Her face..."

Ray didn't answer.

"I thought it was Alex, until I realized he'd consider it beneath him to repeat himself."

"She took everything," Ray said.

"What was she doing? She was up to something. What was it?"

Ray ignored him.

"Answer me!"

"What do you care?" Ray drawled. "What does it matter to you? You tryin' to absolve yourself of this one, or working on something to curse yourself with for the rest o' your life?"

Pritchett curled his lip at the drunken truth of it. "What was she doing?" he asked again.

Ray shook his head. The words barely made it through the haze of liquor. "I don't know. Something with Hannah. I don't know."

"Where's Alex?"

Ray slowly poured himself another. "Gone to Pontchartrain Park, to meet Hannah, I think."

He drank to clear his mind of the image in the mirror: the blood splattered monster, dressing his corpse. He didn't hear Pritchett leave.

"Alex was the one who told me she was there with him." He sat imprisoned by the legs of upturned chairs. "He's the one who told me she had taken everything."

* * * *

"It's time," she said softly.

Deke's eyes popped open. Hannah stood over him. Once she saw he was awake, she left the room. His limbs stuck to the bed like lead weights. His body resisted any prospect of movement. If death meant peace, he would have welcomed it.

Rising, he felt ancient. The pain had no loci. It was everywhere. He dragged himself up anyway.

In the living room, Hannah stood loading a gun. She
barely paused to acknowledge his presence and then resumed
her task. With her black dress now topped with a Sunday go-
to-meeting black hat, she looked very much the widow. Neither said a word as they walked to Hannah's car. The crickets
and cicadas hissed maniacally in the dark. Hannah opened
the trunk and pulled a blanket from it. She threw it in the
back of the car, then slid into the driver's seat. Gingerly,
Deke eased himself into the backseat. He kept low, but not
so low that he couldn't see out the windows. The streets were
almost deserted in these predawn hours. The occasional
stragglers still appeared, alone or in pairs, to accent the night
with their wild costumes. Out here, away from the Quarter,
it was a dark, empty world only dotted with monsters and
harlequins.

A chain of red taillights appeared in the distance. As they
approached, they saw the flashing red and yellow lights of the
police roadblock. Deke pressed himself back against his seat as
if he could reverse their course through sheer will. But Hannah
drove on.

"Get down," she said.

Deke dropped down to the car floor and covered himself
with the blanket. He couldn't see a thing, but he felt the car
stop, then move forward a few feet, then stop again and move
forward again, as slowly it approached the barricade. Hannah
watched as the car in front of her received a thorough search.
She turned around, and yes, the cars lined up behind her
blocked any escape. She pulled the lace veil down over her
face. Deke thought he'd lost his mind when he heard small
sobs coming from the front of the car.

The cop approached Hannah's window and shined a flashlight in her face. Through her veil, he saw the tears.

"What's the problem, ma'am?"

"I'm sorry," Hannah sobbed. "My husband . . . I just came from the hospital . . . He's died. He's been killed. I'm just on my way home."

"I'm sorry to hear that ma'am. I just need to take a quick look at your license."

"Of course." Hannah rummaged in her purse and pulled out the license.

"We're looking for a murder suspect," the cop explained. "You haven't seen any suspicious people, or anyone walking or hitching up this road, have you?"

"No, officer. I'm afraid I wouldn't have noticed if there had been."

Another cop approached the first. He too looked at Hannah's license, and then whispered feverishly to the first.

"I'm so sorry, ma'am. I didn't recognize you . . . realize . . ." the cop blurted. "Go right on through. I'm so sorry."

"Of course, officer. Thank you."

"Would you like an officer to drive you home, ma'am?" the second cop offered. "You must be mighty upset."

"No, thank you—"

"Really, it wouldn't be no problem."

"No, please—"

"We could escort you if you like—"

Deke could have shot the little kiss-ass right then and there.

"That's fine," Hannah said with a hint of steel. "I'm fine."

The cop backed off. "You drive carefully now." Hannah pulled the car forward. After a safe distance, Deke climbed out from under his blanket. He caught Hannah's eye in the rearview mirror. He couldn't help but admire her.

* * * *

Pritchett arrived at the amusement park gate. He noticed the brightly lit midway and animate rides. They had to be inside, he thought. He studied the tall fence and flashed back to his boyhood: Grabbing two handfuls of chain link, he began hoisting himself up. He cleared the top without snagging himself on its spikes. Only on the descent did he lose his footing and take a fall.

He had watched them haul Stacy's body out of the hotel with a sheet concealing her disfigured face. His job had always been to maintain order. Warning Moreau should have preserved order, not unleashed chaos. If only Stacy were dead and Moreau were still alive, he would not have felt compelled to come. He would have rested easier. That would have made sense. He wanted it all to make sense. In his guilt and grief he reverted to what, at heart, he'd always been—fastidious clerk. Only this time, he was keeping death's records instead of Moreau's.

Pritchett had been swallowed by the dark beyond the midway by the time Hannah's car arrived at the park. When the car stopped, Deke hauled himself out of the backseat and looked around.

"You wait here," Hannah said. As she walked away, she ripped the widow's hat from her head and threw it to the ground. Deke leaned against the car, then sat back down on the seat. It was cool, but he was sweating. Dizzy again, he lay back and closed his eyes.

At the gate, Hannah saw the cut chain and knew Alex was there. She closed the gate behind her before heading down the midway.

"Hello, Hannah."

She jumped and turned to see Pritchett standing there. Her relief ran neck and neck with her annoyance.

"Go home, Pritchett."

"Stacy's dead." Hannah hadn't known about Stacy. She stopped for an instant to decide if it mattered. It didn't.

"What is this?" Pritchett asked.

She stared blankly at him.

"What is happening?" he demanded, unnerved by that stare on her face.

She turned to walk away. He grabbed her.

"Answer me!"

She stopped. She turned slowly toward him.

"I'm going to do it." she said.

He let go of her. "Do what?"

"Be what I was again."

Pritchett thought for a moment. He studied her face. He was beginning to understand. "Oh, poor Hannah," he said.

"Yes," she smiled, shaking her head in the affirmative.

"It's much too late for that."

The gun slid out of her purse so fluidly that Pritchett barely noticed it.

"You can't say that," she said. "I'll kill you. And them. And no one will know I was here."

"*You'll* know, Hannah."

"I will FORGET!"

The gun pointed at him, Pritchett looked around for an escape. "You're insane," he told her. "Where's Deke?"

She smiled. "He did this to me," she said. "He did it. He said he'd take me *everywhere*. But he led me here—"

"DEKE," Pritchett shouted. "DEKE!"

"SHUT UP!" She lifted the gun higher.

"We can stop it, Hannah. This doesn't have to get any worse."

"No one must know I was here," she said.

"Hannah, let me help you." He reached his hand out to her.

"You should have seen me," she said, in awe, as if amazed herself at what she'd become.

The bang blasted the stillness to pieces. Alex heard the shot and went running from the big top tent to the midway.

Deke heard it too. And then he heard police sirens. He jumped from the car and looked for Hannah. He saw the flashing lights round the corner. He ran to the fence. He looked up and down but couldn't see a gate. The police cars were heading straight for him. He grabbed the fence and, defying every nerve in his body, climbed to the top. He got there, but then his fingers turned to liquid. He slid down the chain link and hit the ground like a rock. Cop cars skidded to stops all around the fence. On his knees and elbows he crawled behind a bush. He didn't think the cops had seen him. Their lights flooded the park. He couldn't move without being seen.

"Deke Watley." His name boomed through a megaphone. "Lay down any weapons and come out." The lights almost blinded him, but he could see that the cops' rifle barrels were pointed toward him. Alex must have told them . . . or Hannah . . .

Alex had ducked inside a technician's shack. When the horn screamed Deke's name, he stepped out. A bullet whizzed past him and blew a hole in the door. He dove back inside. Was that Deke's bullet, or Hannah's? One shot had already sounded. Was someone dead? Who, he wondered, might the luckless bastard have been? Could Deke have figured it out? Could he have come to his senses and put a hole in that pretty little head? Alex slammed through the door and dashed to an empty carnival booth. Earlier, pink bunnies and fuzzy teddy bears would have lined the empty shelves. Now, searching for anything unlucky enough to be alive, bullets

singed the night air. If Hannah was shooting, she was surprisingly good.

Deke broke cover and ran for the dark of the midway as
cannonlike booms shook the air. Fireworks spat from the
cops' rifles as the bullets exploded, very much in keeping with
this town's festive air. Deke fell against the nearest building.
Sweat poured off him. The world spun around.

He crashed through a door and wound up on the floor of a
narrow hallway. When he tried to stand, he fell down again on
the slick, oddly slanted floor. In a flash of light he saw his
image on the wall, freakish and twisted. He crawled to level
ground and pulled himself up. A large foyer offered him five
doors. He chose the one straight ahead and landed in a pitch-
black room. He kept his hand on the doorknob, but he
couldn't see the walls and had no idea how big this dark room
might be. The floor began to spin beneath him. He fell to his
knees. Dim light crept in, and something touched him from
behind. He shot forward, and turned to see a hand outstretched. He gasped, and then he realized where he was. The
house of horrors. He was in a house of horrors. He smiled. He
came pretty damned close to a laugh.

He knew he couldn't stand so he crawled toward . . . toward
what? As the room spun around he looked for the door. There
had to be a door. He ran his hand along the walls, but they
were glassy and smooth, and they twisted and deformed his
reflection as the room spun around. The revolving wall of
mirrors stretched and gnarled him, tore him apart and then
tossed him back together again.

"Deke." He heard a whisper. "Deke, where are you?"

A laugh tore through the room. Other voices followed—
voices chattering and hissing like fishwives telling lurid tales.
Deke lost his bearings. Bloodied and broken faces came out of

the walls. He swatted at unseen hands touching him. Malicious mouths whispered curses in his ears as gunshots tore through his side and a woman he loved beat him with her fists as if she hoped to kill him.

At the same time, Hannah was lost in a mirrored maze. As sick as she was of bumping her nose on her own reflection, she was ready to shoot through the fucking glass. That's what she did when she heard Deke screaming. A thousand tiny Hannahs flew through the air when her first bullet struck.

When the shards had settled, she was no better off. No passageways. No door. So she shot again, and again, in every direction, and in the hail of shattered glass, the blizzard of glistening daggers, and she saw thousandfold a perfect image of herself flying and falling to the ground.

Then she saw the door. Exposed, it seemed to mock her for having failed to see through its disguise. She opened it.

"Don't go near her," a disembodied voice warned Deke. The walls might as well have been talking. "If you kill me, she'll feed you to those cops. She has to. It was all her idea. Bringing you here. Using you . . ."

The room stopped spinning. His scream had done it. As soon as the scream died, the spinning slowed like a top winding down. If that was all his tormentors wanted—a little terror, capitulation—Deke would have offered it up a long time ago. Finally motionless, Deke could think. The dizziness almost subsided. Only the pain stayed right where it was.

"Liar!" a voice hissed. Deke could no longer tell which voices were real.

"Hannah!" he called. He wanted her to tend him as she'd done before. He wanted to hold her. He wanted the girl in the yellow dress who'd always loved him.

His gun drawn, Alex crept along the narrow halls. Inching

forward through another set of fun-filled corridors, Hannah eyed every crevice and corner, waiting for Alex's face to pop up like a jack-in-the-box. She jumped and screamed like a schoolgirl when a gorgon's head, its hair of snakes undulating and accusatory, shot out from the wall. She raised the gun and blasted the prop. Wires sizzled; papier-mâché dusted the air. She reloaded while she waited for her heart to quit pounding.

Deke finally found the rectangular outline that marked the door. He staggered toward it and stepped through. He got back to the slanted entryway. When he opened the outside door, a cop was standing not twenty feet from him. He froze until the cop turned away. It had started to rain.

He ducked back inside and shut the door. He knew where he'd just come from; he knew where he didn't want to be. He had four other choices. His first impulse was to take the door on the right. So Deke went left. As soon as he stepped into what should have been his haven, he heard a shot. It was no ordinary gunshot, and by now, to Deke, there were such things as ordinary gunshots. This one boomed like monstrous tower bells. He put his hands to his ears to stop the pressure from the weight of that sound.

"Find him, Deke." And then a thousand times: "Find him . . . Find him . . . He's trying to kill me . . . me . . . me . . ." The words echoed endlessly.

"You're doing . . . doing . . . the killing, Hannah . . . Hannah." Another shot boomed and crashed into the wall. Hugging the edge of the room, Deke slid away into the dark. When he felt another knob, he turned it and pushed through. He tripped on a step and then landed outside in the mud; the steady rain splattered him. He scampered to his feet and ran across the midway. Hearing him, a cop hurried over. His gun ready, the cop looked inside the open door. He saw Deke's muddy tracks and followed them.

Through the same door Hannah came running as if it were broad daylight and she were hailing a cab. She still held her purse aloft, the object as dainty and refined as the gesture, while in her other, the gun stood ready. The cop turned when he heard her. Rain plastered Hannah's wild yellow hair in thick strands to her head. The cop paused when he saw a woman; he shouldn't have. The purse dangling from her wrist, she took the gun in both hands and held her arms outstretched. She screamed when she pulled the trigger. She didn't know why. The scream just happened. It also heralded the cop's death as the blood spread across on his chest.

"Over here!"

Feet smacked the muddy ground as cops converged on her.

"Hannah!"

She spotted Deke's head poking from beneath a shiny black tarp. She ran to him, and he lifted the tarp to let her in. Neither breathed as the cops ran toward their fallen comrade. Silent and still, Deke kept his eye on the police outside. Hannah slowly eased her gun toward him, her finger on the trigger. Deke lifted the tarp; something caught his eye. Hannah looked too. Across the midway, at the entrance to the theatrical tent stood Alex. He looked right at them, then disappeared inside.

"Come on," Deke said.

"You go," she told him. "You've got to kill him."

He looked down and saw her gun pointed his way.

"Come on!" he demanded. He grabbed her arm and lifted the tarp. The cops were hauling the wounded man away. Deke and Hannah quietly crossed the rain-soaked midway. Still holding Hannah's arm, Deke parted the tent's flaps and pulled her inside. It was completely dark in there. They didn't move.

Deke shielded his face when a huge spotlight blinded him. Hannah didn't flinch.

"KILL HIM!" she screamed, shooting wildly. She hit the spotlight and the room fell dark again.

"Tell him, Hannah. You might as well. Let the man die in peace." Another spotlight blared down on Hannah. And then another, and another, until she stood trussed in light from all directions.

"Take a good look, Deke," Alex said.

"Kill him." Deke didn't move. "For *us!*"

"She killed my father." Deke saw a silhouette up on the stage. "We had it planned. You were the fall guy. Then she decided to get rid of me as well. She let you go, so you could come here and do it. She called the cops so they could pick you up afterwards. But now, with a dead cop outside, they'll step aside—no unnecessary chances, you know. Just cart the bodies out when it's over."

Soaked and filthy, she stood encased in the light. "LIAR!" she shrieked and raised her gun at the blinding spot. Before she could fire, all the lights died. The dark again. Deke moved forward. He didn't know where Hannah was. Suddenly a whole bank of stage spots blazed. Alex's silhouette ruled the stage. Although Alex stood motionless, a human form obscured in light, something in his posture alerted Deke. Alex spoke not a word, offered no gesture, and yet . . . Deke turned. Hannah stood with her arms outstretched toward him—the loaded gun pointed at his heart.

"I loved you," she said.

"Hannah, no."

"How could you have thought well of her?" Alex asked.

"I knew her," he said.

She looked up at that stage as if the grail itself were there for the taking, as if all reason and goodness would be restored were it not for Alex alive up there. She had watched his mother die. She'd heard the fight and hid in the next room. She'd stood there, immobilized with fear, amazed, while Alex, a child, watched that dog and that nigger witch mutilate things. And she hadn't moved a muscle—just watched and drunk in the horrors—watched Alex's mother rip out Moreau's eyes as if they were jewels encased in an otherwise worthless statue. Hannah watched. And seeing it was like having handcuffs slapped on her wrists that bound her interminably to all this filth.

"Kill him," she told Deke. "Then you and I can go away. That's what you wanted, isn't it?"

Deke watched her. She was the same. That's what shocked him. He couldn't say he didn't know her. He couldn't say she had changed. She hadn't. This was Hannah. He still saw the innocence there. He was not mistaken. He had just gotten innocence wrong. There was no goodness or purity in it. Innocence was wanting a thing, and not knowing why, and raging because you couldn't have it.

"Kill him," she said, a plea in her voice.

He stared at her gun, at her face, at the past. He saw his life and his world in her, everything he'd run from and everything he'd feared. She was all of it, standing there, and he couldn't disguise his revulsion at what had become of the whole damned thing.

"Don't look at me like that." The plea disappeared, and the hatred flared. She marched toward him and waved the gun in his face.

"Look at me like you used to," she said. She smacked the butt of her gun against his face. "GO ON!"

He licked the blood from his lip. He'd just gotten innocence wrong.

Hannah stepped back. "I'll kill you . . ." she said softly "and him . . ." She paused. "And no one will know I was here."

She took careful aim at Deke. Her hand squeezed the barrel, and her finger pressed the trigger.

He teetered a moment. He looked down at the blood on his shirt, but couldn't tell the old from the new. Then he looked at Alex, as if he were the one who had pulled the trigger. Again she raised the gun, and another shot ripped through him.

As Deke's blood seeped out of him, the fat man's florid face from the bus ride filled his vision. *"Before that, though,"* he'd said through a lewd smile, *"before that they go just a little bit crazy."* Deke fell to his knees and took his head into his hands, as if amazed at what he hadn't seen and what he hadn't known. He desperately sucked air into his lungs. He looked at Hannah with terror in his eyes. He reached toward her and she stepped aside to avoid his grasping hand. Images of her ran through his mind: her outstretched arms leaning against the jukebox, her eyes closing when he laid his palm against her face. Her first honest-to-goodness laugh since he'd found her again. Falling into his arms to the strains of "Lonely Woman."

He slumped down into the dirt.

Alex watched. He let the gun fall to his side. He thought about killing her right then. Somehow, though—and if he'd had presence of mind, he would have laughed at the thought—somehow, it just didn't seem sporting. He stepped out of the light. He watched Deke roll onto his back. He watched Deke's chest heave; he watched him choke on the intake of air, then desperately exhale.

"He didn't deserve that," Alex said.

"Neither did I," she replied.

There was a pause.

"Now?" he asked.

"I have to get away," she said. She tore her eyes away from Deke. "Let me go."

They both noticed the stillness. Deke's chest no longer lurched up and down. It was quiet. They both held their breath a moment, to see if the movement would resume. It did not.

Alex breathed again. His father was dead. The assigned killer was dead. He was free. For the first time he breathed the air of not having to fight. That one last death, and he no longer had to fight. He thought of the last time he and Hannah had stood over a bloody corpse. It had been his mother's; and it marked the beginning. Now, how fitting an end.

"Officially," he said, "you've shot the man who killed your husband. They won't touch you."

He walked toward the exit.

"Let me go," she said and pointed her gun at him.

He stopped; he cocked his head as if he wasn't quite sure of what he'd heard. He raised his hands a bit.

"Go then," he said.

"Your father . . ." she began, then fell silent.

"My father's dead."

"He made me stay."

"I know."

"He said he'd have me put away if I didn't. I killed a man, you know, after he left me." She nodded toward Deke.

"You've killed several, Hannah."

"No one must know I was here."

And then he saw. From the stage, he'd heard her voice, but hadn't seen her face. Now, up close, he saw.

"You're really quite insane, you know?"

"You're the last who knows I was here."

She lifted her gun. Alex did not move. The blast came from

nowhere. The pain . . . rent flesh and blood and bone—a revelation of pain. And Alex had not moved. She still stood and, staring at him open-mouthed, wondered what magic he had used to do this to her. Then Jimmy appeared, gun in hand. He kept his eye on the gun she was still holding, but without the strength to point it anywhere. As she stood, reeling, Jimmy put his gun in Deke's lifeless hand. Hannah watched.

Alex studied her death. He should have cared. He'd seen this face for most of his life; the least he could do was bear witness. Just before she died, he knelt and looked down at her. She grasped his hand. He let her, because, for the first time, he didn't have to fight. Her grip was strong, and it seemed to grow even stronger the closer she came to dying. Suddenly, her familiarity struck him. He had seen her every day—all of his life. He hesitated a moment, then reached down and stroked her head. The feel of her skin was sudden and strange. In all these years, he had never touched her. She closed her eyes at that, and she died.

He stood over her body. Hannah had wanted to be what she was again. Alex considered that he had no sweet yesterdays to return to. He looked at the bodies lying on the ground and thought of where he'd been, what he'd done . . . the whole bloody tango his mother and father forced him to finish for them . . . the stench and the din of this town . . . He would go away, of course. He had found a place where a half-black man could buy some peace, and each day, at least once, he figured, he would have a waking nightmare of where he'd been and what he'd done to get it.

Jimmy signaled that it was time to go. Alex took one last look. He would not make her mistake of trying to forget, he thought, as he headed toward the back of the stage. Between the black and the white, there had never been any innocence in him.